TWO HEARTS DANCING

"You begin to make me regret accepting this dance with you."

"Don't make it seem as if it were my idea. You were throwing yourself in my way the moment I entered the room."

"Throwing myself—!" Roslyn did not often find herself speechless. "Under the circumstances, I choose to forgive your rudeness. You can't help feeling jealous."

"Jealous?"

"Yes, because I'm first to the altar, not you." She eyed him speculatively. "What did you believe I meant—that I thought you were jealous because I was marrying someone other than yourself? I'm not so presumptuous, my lord."

"You relieve me." He laughed, but it was not the warm, hearty laugh she loved to hear.

"We came close, though, didn't we?" she said, allowing her tone to wax sentimental. "You were eleven, I think, when you tendered your first proposal."

"And why didn't you accept?"

"The thought of having you dictating to me at all times was daunting, to say the least."

His laughter was genuine this time. "But you changed your mind later, didn't you?"

Her answering smile faded as she recalled the period during her adolescent years when she had mistakenly believed she loved him. "All young girls go through a time of madness when they're growing up," she cried, scowling at him. A light suddenly sparkled in her eyes as she performed the next few steps atop his immaculate boots.

He grunted and stumbled, then swung her around at arm's length. "Poor, poor Jonathan." He brought her closer to him and lowered his voice, as if unwilling to allow anyone dancing past to hear his words. For an instant his cravat rubbed against her cheek, and her foolish skin flushed at the contact. "Does he know what he's letting himself in for, marrying you . . . ?"

Also by Marcy Stewart

THE BRIDEGROOM AND THE BABY
LADY SCANDAL
THE VISCOUNT TAKES A WIFE
DARBY'S ANGEL
LORD MERLYN'S MAGIC
MY LORD FOOTMAN
CHARITY'S GAMBIT

Novellas in Anthologies:

"An Indefinite Wedding"
in FLOWERS FOR THE BRIDE
"Lady Constance Wins" in LORDS AND LADIES
"A Halo for Mr. Devlin"
in SEDUCTIVE AND SCANDALOUS
"The Enchanted Bride" in MY DARLING BRIDE

Published by Zebra Books

A BRIDE FOR LORD BEAUMONT

Marcy Stewart

Zebra Books
Kensington Publishing Corp.

http://www.zebrabooks.com

ZEBRA BOOKS are published by

Kensington Publishing Corp.
850 Third Avenue
New York, NY 10022

Zebra and the Z logo Reg. U.S. Pat. & TM Off.

First Printing: April, 2000
10 9 8 7 6 5 4 3 2 1

Printed in the United States of America

*Dedicated to the East Tennessee Romance Writers,
for their constant support, encouragement, and
priceless friendship*

One

Standing in the center of a cluster of guests, Roslyn Andrews thought her twenty-first birthday ball must be the best celebration ever seen at Misthaven; perhaps even in the entire village of Chawton. The May night in Hampshire was as perfect as if she'd ordered it from heaven, and a sweet breeze from open windows cooled the whirling dancers. The servants had decorated perfectly, and the food was excellent. Most of all, the vibrant conversations, the bursts of laughter from her well-garbed guests seemed genuine, not merely polite. Perhaps they felt her happiness and her father's, for it was no secret that her betrothal would soon be announced. Everyone loved a wedding. Everyone loved romance.

As for herself, she could not be happier.

Hidden by the folds of her ball gown, her fingers tapped a rhythm totally at odds with that of the orchestra.

Well, if she were to be honest with herself, there was one thing, or rather one *person*, who had yet to appear, and then her happiness would be complete. Vexed, she scanned the elegant dancers swirling past, the scores of friends and neighbors sitting or standing in groups against the gilded walls. No luck. Tilting her head, she could barely see the hall and the few guests milling about, but he was not there either.

"If you're searching for your soon-to-be-betrothed," Roslyn's father told her in a low voice, "he's dancing with the vicar's wife."

"I know," she said, and distractedly handed her dance card to a middle-aged gentleman who had asked her to reserve the *allemande* for him. "I suggested that he ask her."

As the last of Roslyn's admirers drifted away, Thurmond Andrews drew his daughter aside before more could take their place. "Then who *are* you looking for? All evening you've been gawking like a child searching for the peanut vendor at a circus."

She smiled. "I suppose I *have* been wondering where Miles is. He said he'd come."

"Oh, Lord Beaumont," said her father, chuckling dismissively. "If he said he'll be here, then he will. Fine old Miles, the brother you never had."

"Well, he's not like a brother precisely . . ."

"Of course he is. You never had siblings, so you don't know. Most certainly no sister and brother could have outdone you in quarrels, but that's to be expected since you were practically raised in each other's pockets."

"As you say, Father," she said with a little frown. She didn't want to argue the point, but no one seemed less like a relative to her than the young viscount.

It was true they had grown up in one another's shadow, but that was because his estate lay across the road from Misthaven and sprawled eastward for approximately two miles. Their fathers had been inseparable from their own youths until the death of Miles's sire two years before. Thus the children had been thrown together often, but that did not make them siblings. Had her father said *friend*, or even occasional *enemy*, that would have been more the thing. Miles would make a horrible brother. He was too rigid, too convinced of the rightness of his own opinion in every matter. He was . . . he was insufferable.

But only sometimes. At other moments he could make her laugh as no one else could. They had shared the great events of each other's lives. If he did not come tonight, she would be crushed with disappointment. And angry. So angry that she would never forgive him.

Unless he'd had an accident. Could one have an accident merely crossing a country road?

She was saved further imaginings by the entrance of a dignified, slender gentleman in black who surveyed the crowd impassively (hating it, she thought with a giggle; Miles detested large gatherings). Although the silver threads of his waistcoat lent a festive air to his formal attire, he nevertheless appeared austere. She wanted to laugh aloud with relief and a kind of pity that he could not, or *would* not, look more congenial.

Many heads turned when he entered, Roslyn

noted, for the viscount was as well known as he
was striking with his dark hair and penetrating
blue eyes. A few guests went out of their way to
greet him, but not as many as Roslyn would have
liked. Yet what could one expect? He'd brought
it on himself. Half the people in the village were
afraid of him and his sharp tongue.

Naturally Miles would never admit that as a
fault of his own. He'd only say something about
his inability to tolerate foolishness or sloppy thinking. She had heard such comments from him all
her life. He was a hopeless creature.

But he was here. Murmuring her pardons to
her father, she made her way through the crowd
to Miles. Something across the room had snared
his attention; but as she approached, he seemed
to sense her presence and slowly turned. She felt
the familiar old *frisson* that warned of battles to
come. In his eyes she recognized an answering
spark.

She greeted him smoothly, giving no sign of her
former worry. He was equally cool as he bowed
over her hand and brought it to his lips, his gaze
never leaving hers. She shivered when he kissed
the small area of her hand that her lacy gloves
did not cover. It was the first time since they were
children that he had actually kissed her, and the
unexpectedness of it made her wary and a trifle
piqued. She thought a boxer might feel similarly
injured if his opponent struck before he was
ready.

"You look very beautiful," he said.

He sounded sincere, but one never knew with Miles. She thanked him as if he had meant it.

In the seconds after he released her hand, neither one spoke. The previous dance ended, and the orchestra began a waltz. Disturbed by their strange awkwardness, Roslyn seized upon it.

"They have begun a waltz, Miles."

"So it would seem." He glanced at the dancers converging on the ballroom floor, then back at her. "What, you mean you haven't a partner?"

She made a pretense of checking her card. "I believe I reserved this one for Mr. Thorne, but he seems to have forgotten." She nodded toward an elderly gentleman seated in a chair against the wall. His head was tipped back and his mouth open in snores that could be heard above the violins. It was a lie. Gregory Burnsmith, a young solicitor, had signed for this dance and was now approaching. Before he could reach her, she guiltily clutched her companion's arm and led him down the three shallow steps to the dance floor.

Though a wry look drifted into his eyes, Miles acceded gracefully enough and swept her into the circle of dancers. "I'm surprised you're not waltzing with Jonathan."

"I've danced several with him already." Fearing her tone sounded less than ecstatic, she searched for the tall presence of Jonathan Leffew, her intended. In the whirling background she saw him standing with a group of gentlemen near the rail that edged the dance floor, trading masculine estate talk, she imagined, or discussing horseflesh or hunting. In the instant she spotted him, the group broke into loud laughter. Jonathan, catching her eye, raised his glass of rum punch and sent her a warm smile. The dear man, she thought, melting. How her father loved him, and not only because her bridegroom's fortune would save their estate. Everyone loved Jonathan. "And besides, he's busy," she told Miles.

"How fortunate I am to have caught you at a propitious moment. Every gentleman will want to dance with the fairest lady in the room."

Her heart tripped a few beats. "You never give me compliments, Miles, and that's the second one in as many minutes."

"Are you keeping score? I only mean to be kind to the bride-to-be. I haven't missed the announcement, have I?"

"No, but had you been much later you would have. Father wanted to speak at the start of the ball, but I wouldn't allow it." She winced, realizing her mistake too late.

"You made him wait for me? I'm astonished. Surely you don't need my approval for your forthcoming alliance."

"I don't! I only wanted you to be in attendance, since you're my friend and closest neighbor."

"Your friend and closest neighbor," he repeated quietly. A slow, mischievous light grew in his eyes. "I believe you're fibbing. You want my blessing, admit it."

"How you make me laugh! Why should I need your blessing, or your approval, or even an opinion? You have nothing whatsoever to do with how I plan to live my life."

She was so indignant that she lost the steps of the dance and stood clumsily for a second until Miles started her going again.

"Come now, Roslyn. You've always consulted my opinion on the major things in your life: which saddle to choose, what color is most stylish for your gig, should you drown your unfortunate, unloved cat or give her away . . ."

"I was no more than a babe when I threatened that, and even then you knew I would never go through with it."

"I'm not so sure. You have a murderous gleam in your eyes at times. Shall I waltz you closer to a mirror so you can see for yourself?"

"I thought on this night at least you could be civil. You begin to make me regret accepting this dance with you."

"Don't make it seem as if it were my idea. You gave me little choice, throwing yourself in my way the moment I entered the room."

"Throwing myself—!" She did not often find herself speechless, but on this occasion taut seconds passed before a means to strike occurred. "Under the circumstances, I choose to forgive your rudeness. You can't help feeling jealous."

"Jealous?"

"Yes. Because I'm first to the altar, not you." She eyed him speculatively. "What did you believe I meant—that I thought you were jealous because I was marrying someone other than yourself? I'm not so presumptuous, my lord."

"You relieve me." He laughed. It was not the warm, hearty laugh she loved to hear, the one that always kindled a similar response in herself. Still, she forced her lips into a smile.

"We came close once, though, didn't we?" she said, allowing her tone to wax sentimental. Tonight it seemed important to speak of the old days, to clear away unresolved issues, for soon it would be too late. Married ladies could not talk of such things, surely. "You were eleven, I think, when you tendered your first proposal."

"That was no proposal. It was an attempt to soften you into giving me one of Silvermane's colts."

"It was a proposal," she asserted.

His grin wavered, and for a moment she imagined she saw vulnerability. "If you believed so, then why didn't you accept?"

"I was eight years old, Miles. The thought of having you dictating to me at all times and never being able to escape was daunting, to say the least."

His laughter was genuine this time. "But you changed your mind later, didn't you?"

Her answering smile faded as she recalled the period during her adolescent years when she had mistakenly believed she loved him. Those were the days he attended Eton and Oxford and came home only occasionally. At each break from school he appeared more mature, more exciting, and very worldly. Apparently he found *her* increasingly childish, for he treated her like an unwanted pest, especially when he brought friends home from university. She had made a dreadful fool of herself on several occasions, and believed those memories would remain painful to her dying day.

Almost as bad was the time that came afterward, when he'd finished school and discovered she was a presentable young lady after all. Miles had actually paid her a few calls, the kind a suitor might. Every conversation had ended in an argument. He had in mind the sort of woman he esteemed, and appeared fixed on sculpting her into that mold. Roslyn was just as determined to remain *herself*.

Moreover, he was so occupied in trying to improve her that he neglected to exhibit the minimum requirements of romance. *A young woman with stars in her eyes needs gentle words in her ears,* she believed. *She needs to think her beloved requires her presence to breathe.* Miles acted as if she *prevented* him from breathing.

His visits became less and less frequent.

And thank goodness they had. Only imagine what could have happened. Instead of this grand night in which would be announced her betrothal to the finest man in all England, she might have fallen into a less felicitous union. She and Miles had tested the possibility of a deeper relationship as one would tiptoe to the edge of a cliff and, finding the plunge too fraught with danger, slip cautiously back.

When she felt certain her voice would remain steady, she said, "All young girls go through a time of madness when they're growing up. You were the only boy close to my age who lived near enough for me to see on a regular basis. I had no one with which to compare you, so naturally my interest fell upon you."

"Yes, I suppose that's true. Jonathan was around, of course, but there is that abominable age difference. Until recently you could have been nothing more than a child to him. And surely he seems—I mean, *seemed* —like someone's uncle to you."

"You're making him sound ancient and he's only thirty. That's still *quite* young."

"True. When you were born, he was a lad of nine. When you were nine, he was already a man."

"Oh!" she cried, scowling at him. A light suddenly sparkled in her eyes as she performed her next few steps atop his immaculate boots.

He grunted and stumbled, then swung her around at arm's length. "You did that deliberately," he accused.

"I cannot dispute you."

"Poor Jonathan. Poor, poor Jonathan." He brought her closer to him and lowered his voice, as if unwilling to allow anyone dancing past to hear his words. "Does he know what he's letting himself in for, marrying you?"

For an instant his cravat rubbed against her cheek, and her foolish skin flushed at the contact. "He will never provoke me as you do, Miles."

"I suppose not." He gazed into the distance, a pensive look on his face.

They danced without speaking for one full circle around the room. The musicians would soon conclude the waltz, Roslyn thought, and she felt overwhelmed with sadness. It could not be that she still had a *tendre* for Miles; naturally such emotion had died long ago. It was only that a part of her life was ending forever. Existence with Jonathan Leffew promised to be better than anything she had known before, but one always felt bereft at endings.

"It would never have worked, you and me," Miles murmured near her ear. The faint scent of his cologne brought her close to tears.

"No. No, it wouldn't have. We cannot get along."

Roslyn made an effort to look at her surroundings and meet the curious stares of the dancers flowing around her. She saw only blurs of shining teeth and flashes of crimson draperies at the long windows, and couldn't force herself to appear as carefree as she knew she should.

Miles finally broke the quiet. "And knowing that, it would be useless to advise you to wait in making the announcement of your betrothal."

His words were spoken so carefully that her heart almost stopped. Their gazes locked. It seemed to her that he had never looked this unsure of himself, or so full of longing. When she answered, she hardly recognized her own voice, so timid did she sound.

"Would there be a reason for me to delay?"

"Would you if there were?"

She felt suspended, caught between the blue of his eyes and the bottomless sea of her own desires. And then, among all the dizzying glimpses of people available in the room, her glance steadied on Jonathan. He was leaning casually against the rail, but his eyes followed her with muted adoration.

"Jonathan . . ." she breathed, the name coming to her lips before she could prevent it.

The spell was broken. "Yes. Jonathan," said Miles. "A fine man." She heard no guile in her partner's tone, only honesty and a trace of regret, and perhaps she imagined the regret. "You couldn't disappoint him."

"Our betrothal is essentially made and lacks only the announcement to make it formal. Everyone knows. To fail to go forward would be . . ."

"Humiliating for him." Miles's lashes lowered in that condescending way he had.

"Precisely. And he's far too kind a man for that sort of treatment."

"True. And such behavior would lack honor."

"Yes, it would. Especially when there's no definite reason for me to do so . . ."

She allowed her words to trail away as she waited, not breathing, for him to disagree. Instead, he murmured an assent, sounding much restored.

"Indeed, Jonathan is the perfect match for you. He hasn't an enemy on earth and is wealthy enough for any bride. He'll be able to restore the Andrews estate to its former glory, and I know that means much to your father. No one else of my acquaintance has the means to do that."

A silence chasmed between them. Roslyn recalled the delight on her father's face when Jonathan first began to court her. After each of those visits, Thurmond Andrews would mutter—partly in jest, but mostly in hope—of new stables, repairs to the roof, updated furnishings, lands to be reclaimed that were currently leased. He had not hidden his wishes for an instant; and she, ever eager to grant him solace following the untimely death of her mother ten years ago, had floated along with his desires.

Now she could not help remembering that Miles had been present more than once when her father spoke so glowingly of her suitor. For the first time it occurred to her that the viscount might have taken discouragement from the fact that his own estate, while not floundering like Misthaven, needed all of its revenues to maintain itself. Her heart quickened with distress.

"Beside all that," Miles was saying, "it won't matter to him what his wife does or doesn't do."

Her heartbeat abruptly slowed. Dangerous eyes lifted to his. After a moment she said, "What do you mean?"

"Well." He laughed lightly, then apologized when they bumped into another couple. "There is a certain image one carries of the ideal wife. When a woman is blessed with the advantage of means, society has certain expectations of her—"

"Society or *you*?"

"—expectations of how she should behave. For instance, she should treat her husband with respect and not contradict him constantly."

"Act the puppet, you mean?" she asked, her lips drawing thin.

"Of course not, but no man wants to think he's marrying a member of a debating team."

"Wed such a woman, Miles, and you'll be bored to suicide," she warned.

"And not only that," he continued, "but a lady should act in a certain manner toward those less fortunate. I'm not speaking of puppets but of the tender and soft type of lady who ministers to the sick and poor. Such a woman brings praise to herself and her household, which is not to diminish the benefits she brings to others."

His mother again, Roslyn thought, glaring at him. Lady Beaumont was an example a saint would have difficulty imitating. Every day she visited the sick and infirm on her estate, bringing baskets of delicacies, herbs for medicines, and anything that was required to alleviate suffering.

Roslyn felt too irked to remind him that her father had improved the cottages of their laborers and instituted better medical care for them only at her urging. She would feel unnatural imitating the personal acts of kindness Lady Beaumont performed, and believed the servants would suspect her of patronizing them if she did. It did no good to remind Miles of these things, for she'd told him of her feelings in the past. He was too inflexible to understand there were different ways of expressing oneself. It was rather pathetic to be so limited.

Instead of snapping at him as was her first desire, she said instead, truthfully, "I admire your mother very much."

"She's an excellent example for us all."

The waltz ended to gentle applause. With a polite expression on her face, Roslyn began to move away, but Miles touched her arm briefly, staying her.

"I haven't wished you a happy birthday," he said.

Roslyn murmured her thanks and again turned away. She could not tolerate one more moment with him.

"I left your present with the butler. It's a whip with a silver handle. Whether you use it on Northwind or to keep your husband in line is for you to decide, though I think only your mare will need it. Jonathan is biddable enough as he is."

She bared her teeth at him and pushed her way to the stairs. The sound of his laughter put her in mind of the baying of a lone, ill-tempered wolf.

Jonathan greeted her as if she'd been gone a month, pressing her hands within his large ones and smiling. No woman could remain vexed long when such an attractive, intelligent gentleman rested his attention upon her.

He was not perfectly handsome, as his nose was rather large and his features craggy. Yet the gentleness of his expression brought much appeal to his visage. A shock of straight hair perpetually fell across his forehead, giving him a boyish look despite its gray streaks, and his brown eyes were as liquid and warm as hot chocolate.

"You looked . . . incredibly lovely just now," he said. "Waltzing . . . with Lord Beaumont."

"How kind of you to say so, Jonathan."

"You both seemed . . . intense."

"Oh." She waved her fingers dismissively, noticed her gloves, then colored as she remembered

Miles's kiss. "We were speaking mainly of his mother."

"You danced well together. But then . . . any man would be improved by your beauty and grace."

How she loved his manner of speaking. Words, uttered in a seductive baritone, fell reluctantly from his lips, making the most mundane pronouncement sound intimate. His voice seldom rose above a husky whisper, yet one did not have to strain to hear him.

Roslyn's responses were delivered in comparably low tones, making her instantly calmer. Jonathan had that effect on her. She adored him for his peaceful manner and believed she was a better person when with him. Their union promised to be a bright one, so very companionable.

She continued to muse as her father drew her and Jonathan to the head of the room. Since the orchestra contained only strings and no brass instruments, the musicians repeated staccato chords as a fanfare. The guests gathered expectantly. Her thoughts seemed to speed and grow as loud as the music—*accelerando, crescendo!*

As her worried eyes scanned the crowd, she visualized the long years ahead with Jonathan wherein the two of them would murmur and smile, murmur and smile. If they were to be blessed with children, their progeny would be known for quiet manners and respectable ways. Eons from now, when she grew aged and death finally came, she would without doubt greet it politely from force of habit.

At the moment her father began to speak, Roslyn's glance found Miles. There was no cynical cast to the viscount's expression now, no sardonic smile. He returned her look with the same measure of solemnity that she felt.

"On this, my one and only child's twenty-first birthday," her father was saying, "I have great tidings—"

"Father!" Roslyn cried.

Thurmond Andrews stopped abruptly, his mouth agape. As the silence expanded, an uncomfortable stirring spread across the room, and curious whispers arose from every side. Roslyn, her heart pounding, felt Miles's gaze slice through her like blue ice. Did she read hope on his face?

And then Jonathan turned to her, his eyes filling with concern and a growing vulnerability that struck her as sharply as a blow.

She could no more wound him than she could kick a puppy. Besides, she loved him. She truly did. Doubts plagued every bride and groom, and though she believed she'd settled hers before accepting this good man at her side, she had allowed fresh ones to overwhelm her for a moment. But no more, no more. She was an Andrews and a lady. She had given her word. And she loved Jonathan Leffew; who could not love him?

"N-nothing, I—I only thought perhaps it would be nicer if the first violinist would play quietly as you speak." With a final, sorrowing glance at Miles, she finished breathlessly, "That is all."

Her father's eyebrows lifted humorously. "By all

means," he said, waving toward the surprised musician, who stumbled into an unsteady improvisation. "Tonight is your night, child." And then he went on with it, the words that bound her to Jonathan Leffew forever.

When he finished and the guests responded with hearty applause and cheers, when she and her betrothed were surrounded with individuals speaking their congratulations and shaking Jonathan's hand, she craned to see around them even as she smiled and thanked and otherwise tried to act the beaming bride-to-be. And was rewarded at last with the sight of Miles leaving the room, one hand raised for the butler to bring his hat.

She blinked to keep her tears from falling. No doubt he thought she should have stopped her father from speaking, but what if she had? It wasn't as though Miles would have stepped into the breach. He'd had a lifetime to declare himself if he truly cared for her.

Obviously, he didn't. Otherwise, he would have said something more definitive than his hints and innuendos this evening. She was not the woman for him, because she'd never fit into his narrow-as-a-straw view of the ideal wife. And that, of course, was the reason he had never declared himself. He wanted a *pliable* wife, a mute replica of his beloved mother.

Probably only the prospect of being alone was making him leave her celebration. He should get married himself, and then he'd be all right.

She clutched Jonathan's hand in a rush of happiness and barely registered his responding smile.

That was the solution! Miles needed a wife, a very malleable wife he could remake in his image. And she was precisely the person to find him one.

Two

On the morning following the ball, the viscount descended the marble stairway of his home to the entry hall and found his mother, Elise, at the central table arranging flowers in a crystal vase. She looked especially fine in her gray morning gown, and not one silver curl had yet straggled out of place. Given time and today's winds, however, that would soon change, he thought fondly. She cared little for such things.

"How was the ball?" Lady Beaumont asked, and smiled absently when he kissed her cheek.

"The usual crowd." Avoiding her warm, lively eyes, he conceded, "The celebration went well enough, I suppose. You should have come with me; you might have enjoyed it."

"I'm sure I would have, but I couldn't leave Georgette in her condition."

Miles forestalled a sigh. "Of course. How is she?"

Lady Beaumont's face became beatific. "She and her baby girl are fine. I wish the same could be said for Henry." She laughed. "You won't protest that I gave him two days' grace before returning to the stables, will you, dear? I vow he suffered more during the delivery than his wife did."

The viscount had no objection to this and said so. Lifting the newspaper from the side table, he moved silently toward the dining room. A moment later he heard the rustling of his mother's skirts as she followed.

"Edwin, would you excuse us for a moment?" Lady Beaumont asked the footman, her gaze remaining locked with her son's. The servant bowed and walked from the room. "Something is wrong. What happened last night?"

"Why, nothing. Everything went as expected; Roslyn's birthday was feted and her engagement announced. I left shortly thereafter because I was bored."

"Bored," repeated Elise, nodding thoughtfully. "So the rumors were true. Roslyn is to be married to Mr. Leffew."

"Yes."

"A fortunate man," she murmured.

"Do you think so?"

"I do indeed. Roslyn is beautiful and vivacious. Everyone loves her." She hesitated. "Miles, you aren't upset because Roslyn is getting married, are you?"

He tried to look incredulous. "What could her wedding possibly mean to me?"

"I don't know," she said, and he felt anguish to see the worried look on her face. "But if you are disturbed about it, I'm most sorry for you for not saying something to her before now. There is a type of man who only wants what he cannot have, but I know you're not like that. Yet the effect is the same. It's too late for you and Roslyn. She's bound to Jonathan now."

"I know." The room grew suddenly hot as the injustice of this observation pulsed through his veins. His mother could have no idea of the real truth. *Must* not. "There's nothing to fret about. We didn't suit."

"Oh, my dear," said his mother. "Please tell me you don't love her as your father and I loved each other. Naturally you have affection for her as a friend, but say you haven't lost your heart."

Miles busied himself at the sideboard to prevent his mother seeing his face. Before he'd matured enough to know his heart's truth, he had thought himself in love half a dozen times, but nothing had proved lasting, each episode ending with thoughts of Roslyn. But like the greatest fool who ever lived, he'd believed he had worlds of time in which to declare himself.

It was no wonder his father believed him to be unfettered.

How life flowered with ironies. Just as he matured enough to realize his love for Roslyn ran deeper than a mere childhood infatuation, his sire had made his greatest error in judgment. Had Miles declared himself to the woman he loved prior to that time, his father could not have proposed a solution to the crisis—a crisis his sire had brought upon them all—that would forever obligate his son.

Bitterness struggled with loyalty. His father had been a good man. Even good men made mistakes.

Miles had committed himself to repairing his father's.

The most important point was that his mother could never know. He had sworn his silence.

He shuddered to think how dangerously close he had come to revealing his feelings to Roslyn last night. He was not blind to her tenderness toward him; but by raising questions in her mind about her betrothal, he had been needlessly cruel. Yet he couldn't resist that last opportunity to know if her emotions flowed one tenth as deeply as his.

And now he knew. From the soft, hopeful look in her eyes, he felt certain Roslyn was as conflicted as he.

His cheeks flushed as he recalled dissolving that taut moment between them by retreating behind petty assaults on her generosity. It was true he'd once been troubled by her lack of conformity, but that was when he'd been a shallow, inexperienced youth. Even so, far better that she think him small-minded enough to make unfavorable comparisons between her and his mother than to know the level of shame to which he had truly fallen.

He should never have gone to the ball.

The room, too warm before, now felt as if it might explode into flames. "I'm not sure I understand the kind of love you and Father had," he said stiffly. "I don't know if I'm capable of it."

Roslyn passed the morning at her desk, where she wrote four missives. When she finished, she rang for her maid and strolled to the sitting room window. A misting rain was falling outside, but the weather failed to dampen her sense of satisfaction.

She glanced at the stack of letters on her desk, her eyes crinkling in merriment. Each extended an invitation for a fortnight's visit to celebrate her betrothal. Naturally she couldn't tell her guests the true reason they were being invited, but she'd hinted there would be unattached gentlemen present. That should bring them running.

The trick would be in getting Miles to cooperate. If he suspected her motives, he'd flee without giving himself a chance to fall in love. Surely by inviting Jonathan and his brother Ned to attend the house party, she would deflect the viscount's suspicious nature.

Oh, it was delicious, simply delicious! When presented with an array of the type of females he thought he wanted, Miles would at last understand that he knew nothing about women and less about himself.

The unbidden thought brought a frown. No, she didn't mean that. She *wanted* him to fall in love and be happy. Her actions were motivated solely by the desire to help an old friend.

An old friend who thought she was a heartless shrew.

Her mood began to curl around the edges.

After a warning knock at the door, the maid entered the sitting room. Roslyn asked her to post the letters, then begged her to stay a moment. "Hetta, what do the servants say about me?"

The older woman stared. Seconds later her shoulders moved upward in a faint shrug. "I'm sure I can't speak for others."

"Please, Hetta. Surely they talk of their employers upon occasion. Do they find me difficult?" How she longed to hear a pleasing answer. "Do *you?*" When the servant still hesitated, she said encouragingly, "You may speak freely without fear of making me angry."

"You're no different from most I've served. None of you gentry see us servants as people. We don't have as much worth in your eyes as a stick of furniture."

"You mean more than that to me!"

"I do? Then tell me how many brothers and sisters I have."

"I—I know that your father is still living."

"That's because your papa pensioned him off to roost in one of his cottages and you see him now and then."

Gazing into Hetta's indignant eyes, Roslyn began to wilt. "Well . . . how many brothers and sisters *do* you have?"

"Nary a one." During her tirade, Hetta's posture had stiffened. Now her spine relaxed slightly, and she slipped the letters into her apron pocket. "If that's all, Miss Roslyn, I'll be going now. I've work to do."

"Yes, Hetta," she said faintly. "Thank you."

Although Oakwood Castle lay at a comfortable walking distance from her home, Roslyn ordered the gig brought round after luncheon because of the drizzle. She was anxious to make certain Miles didn't plan to dash off to London or Scotland or some island in the Pacific where beautiful brown-skinned girls wore only grass skirts and flowers in their hair. He must be available at the appropriate time or all would be lost.

As she reined her horse onto the long, paved approach to the viscount's home, she gazed with appreciation at the well-tended grounds and, at the crown of a gentle rise, the Jacobean house with its modest corner turrets, long, symmetrical windows, and gabled portico. Even when veiled in a mist as today, the sight of the estate never failed to move her, not only due to its beauty but because the history of a home older than any in the county fired her imagination. Countless generations of Beaumonts had lived out their loves, delights, and tragedies here.

When she arrived, the butler, Jasper, ushered her into the parlor with the friendliness of long acquaintance, then begged she wait as he summoned the viscount and Lady Beaumont. It might take some moments to find them, he said, and would she like a cup of tea to warm her as she waited?

Roslyn thanked him and sat on a gold brocade sofa near the fire. Moving with quick grace, Jasper stoked the fire and exited. Recalling Hetta's comments, the young lady wondered if the butler resented her, too.

Several moments later, Lady Beaumont entered the room. "What a delight it is to see you," said the lady warmly. "I've missed you, but I know you've been too busy with plans for your ball to pay social calls. And now I understand you're to be married!"

"Miles must have told you." As Lady Beaumont was about to admit the truth of this, Roslyn burst out, "And where is he?"

"Miles? I believe he went for a ride."

"Oh." Roslyn forced herself to brighten, and added, "I had something in particular I wanted to ask of him, but I suppose it will wait."

Jasper entered the room at that moment and served tea to the ladies. When he glided away, Lady Beaumont said, "Do tell me about your wedding plans. Jonathan Leffew is such a fine man, and I know you will make a beautiful couple."

Roslyn raised her gaze. In the other woman's eyes she saw a distant sadness that made her look away. Quickly, Roslyn began to chatter about Jonathan and his proposal. He had been very gallant, she told her hostess. After asking her father's permission, he had taken her on a picnic where they ate pheasant and sipped champagne. At the bottom of her glass she had discovered a sapphire ring. She had been most surprised, especially when Jonathan slipped to one knee and begged her hand in marriage. The park had been quite populated that day, she told Lady Beaumont. Somehow everyone seemed to be watching them with expectant faces. When she finally nodded her acceptance (Roslyn avoided mentioning the long pause that went before it), several of the observers broke into applause.

"How very romantic," said the older woman, studying Roslyn in a manner that made her long to rush from the room.

"Jonathan is . . ." What *was* Jonathan? she suddenly wondered. She had known him for years, but at this instant she could not remember anything about him, not even what he looked like. "Jonathan is very kind," she finished, feeling weak.

"Yes, he is," said a voice from the hall.

Roslyn turned with immediate gladness. Miles nodded and gave her a polite smile as Jasper removed his dripping greatcoat. After running a hand through his damp hair, the viscount entered the room and sat opposite the ladies.

"Is everything well?" he asked Roslyn. "I was surprised to see your gig in the drive so soon after your celebration."

"I've come because I have some exciting news to deliver."

"My heart leaps to hear it, then," he said.

She lowered her lashes, then decided to proceed in spite of his cynical tone. "In celebration of my betrothal, I've invited several of my friends from Montrose for a house party beginning Saturday next."

"Ah, Montrose," he said, leaning back and accepting a cup of tea from Jasper, who hurried from the room after performing this service. "That's a name I've not heard in a few years. Thought you hated that place."

"I did, of course. But I made several lasting friendships at the school."

Miles blew across the top of his cup to cool the steaming liquid. "I thought those young ladies had married. Weren't you in several weddings? Are they bringing their husbands as well?"

"No, I've only invited my unmarried friends."

"The spinsters? Why? Surely you don't mean to gloat that you've found a willing victim and they haven't."

"Miles, for pity's sake!" Lady Beaumont's voice throbbed with amused outrage.

At almost the same time, Roslyn said in deadly tones, "Of course I'm not gloating, and I don't consider them spinsters. They're all lovely, presentable young ladies!"

"Then why such a select group?" he asked.

For a moment, Roslyn was at a loss. While she searched for a logical answer, Lady Beaumont ventured softly, "Are they to be your attendants, my dear?"

"Yes!" the young woman cried gratefully. She didn't know why she hadn't thought of it herself. "They're to be my attendants, and I wish to thank them in advance with a visit to the country. Jonathan and Ned are coming to provide escorts for the various activities I've planned. I'm hoping you'll be available as well."

Miles set his cup on the table. "I'm afraid not."

Roslyn felt her heart drop. "But why?"

"House parties are tedious."

"Oh, but this one won't be," she pleaded. "The guests are young and lively and interesting." Desperately she glanced at Lady Beaumont for help. "Please say you'll join us, Miles. It's not as though you'll be trapped. You have only to walk across the road to go home if you become bored."

Lady Beaumont, her gaze wandering back and forth between them, said slowly, "Why don't you, Miles? It would be a way to help an old friend, one who will be leaving us all too soon."

Roslyn nodded her affirmation and, biting her lower lip anxiously, sent him a look of appeal. Miles turned his eyes to the side with the expression of a man trapped.

"I'll give the matter some thought," he said.

Three

The first reply to Roslyn's invitations came several days after the ball. When the butler brought the missive into the library where Roslyn, her father, and Jonathan were seated, the young lady seized the letter and broke the seal with unseemly haste.

"Oh, Victoria Pendergrass has written to say she can attend the house party!" she exclaimed, thinking, *I knew she'd be first to respond.* Of all her companions at Montrose, Victoria had seemed the most likely to wed first. Certainly if desire led the race, she would have wed first.

Well, perhaps now her ambition would come true. Victoria embodied everything she believed Miles dreamed about: blond, buxom, meek, and agreeable—to the point of insipidity, Roslyn thought wickedly.

Thurmond Andrews cleared his throat and shifted his short, thick frame. "Victoria, Victoria . . . is she the one who laughs like a howling jackal?"

With a chuckle, Roslyn said, "I believe you're thinking of Colleen Sheridan." Colleen had been a member of Roslyn's inner circle, and her frequent laughter and witty comments did much to bind the group together. Roslyn regretted losing touch with the raven-haired girl, and felt a rush of anticipation at seeing her—and indeed, *all* of them—again.

Mr. Andrews folded his newspaper into an untidy rectangle and dropped it on the floor. "How many are we expecting?"

"Only four young ladies, Father; don't worry." Her sire treasured peace and quiet above all things. Sometimes she suspected his joy at her betrothal stemmed more from anticipating having the house to himself than his liking for Jonathan.

"My brother and I are very much looking forward to the gathering," Jonathan said in his slow, lingering way. His gaze rested peacefully on Roslyn, and she gave him a quick smile to acknowledge his support.

"You're a better man than I," Mr. Andrews said. Suddenly his eyes narrowed at her under bushy eyebrows. "What in heaven's name is wrong with your hair, child?"

Roslyn's spirits sank as one hand flew reflexively to her curls. "Don't you like the style? I arranged it myself."

"*Why?* What am I paying Hetta for, if not to make you look decent? You're going to frighten off your fiancé with that thatch."

"I think she looks charming," her betrothed said.

"Thank you, Jonathan," she said in injured

tones. To her father she added, "Hetta is sleeping late this morning."

"Hetta is doing *what*?" cried Mr. Andrews. "Is today Sunday and nobody told me?"

Roslyn's chin lifted. "I think it's important to treat servants well. My maid works very hard for me and deserves time off now and then."

She decided not to mention the looks of shock she'd received from the servants when she brought a cup of hot tea to Hetta's bedside that morning, nor would she recount the maid's avaricious expression upon accepting the offering. The gesture had not brought the satisfied glow she'd anticipated, and she wondered again how Lady Beaumont continued in her good works when the results were so unpredictable.

Flushing with outrage, Mr. Andrews said, "That woman gets a half day off on Sundays like all the other servants. Start treating one differently and you'll have a riot."

"I'm sorry if I've offended you, Father. I thought Hetta was *my* servant and I could make decisions about her myself, but now I see I was mistaken!"

"Now . . ." began Jonathan, blinking in concern as he glanced from daughter to parent and back again. Roslyn and her father stared at him, waiting. The young lady had a sudden premonition: *I shall spend my life tarrying for his gentle pronouncements.* At last he said, "Roslyn, your kindness to your servant does you credit. Yet your father's point about jealousy among the help is a

good one. Perhaps it would be best if your generosity to your maid is a singular occurrence."

"Or we could extend the holiday to include the
other servants," said Roslyn.

"That would be another way of looking at it,"
Jonathan said, his tone neutral.

"No it would not," asserted Mr. Andrews. "I'm
not paying the same wages for less work. The
neighbors would string me up by my ears if I
started such foolishness."

"Servants are people, too, and deserve to be
treated as such," Roslyn said, then fell silent as
Marsden, the butler, entered to replenish their
tea. The silver-haired man's spine seemed even
straighter than usual. Although he normally kept
his eyes downcast when performing his duties, he
sent Roslyn a scalding look that nearly curdled
the blood in her veins.

Over the next few days, Roslyn received two
more acceptances. Colleen Sheridan and Harriet
Pollehn wrote of their anticipation of the upcoming fortnight. Roslyn felt the kind of satisfaction
she imagined a director must feel when all the
elements of a play fall into place. But when the
Thursday before her guests were to arrive rolled
around with no message from Esther Cummings,
she could not help feeling deflated. Her old
friend must be away from home. It was the only
reason she could think why Esther would remain
silent.

That afternoon, sick to death of preparations

and speculations, she escaped on Northwind, her mind heavy with worries.

Esther had been her very best friend at school. Roslyn felt she had been at her most altruistic in asking her to attend. Miles would have to dig both booted heels into the ground to resist Esther's sweetness, she thought as she felt both anticipation and something she feared was regret.

She clicked Northwind into a canter. The feeling was very like flying, she imagined, with the sense of free movement and the wind whipping at her hair. But she knew it was only a sensation that would soon pass.

One other problem was tugging her spirits downward. The household was becoming an increasingly uncomfortable place. When she pulled the cord for service, no longer could she expect an immediate answer. And not only were the servants slow, they responded with impatient looks bordering on insolence. At least twice she had discovered dust on the mahogany furnishings in the parlor, and often the fires went untended, with ashes piling on the hearth like anthills. As a consequence, her father's temper, never very even, flared more often.

If all of this could be attributed to her kindness to Hetta, she was ready to stop. In truth, she'd tried to stop already, ceasing to bring the maid a morning drink and asking that she take more care with her duties. But the damage seemed done. The servant reported so late each day that Roslyn had begun sending her gown to be ironed by the scullery maid and dressing herself. But the scullery maid wasn't any better. Only that morning, Roslyn's favorite carriage dress had been ruined by a scorch mark burned directly over the heart.

Roslyn's inclination was to dismiss Hetta, but she felt an overriding sense of guilt in causing the problem in the first place. Even worse, the maid had been part of their staff for years and had served Roslyn's mother. She couldn't give her the sack, she simply could not. Somehow, some way, she must solve this problem.

Yet tomorrow she expected her guests to arrive, and the servants were cleaning linens and airing the rooms with sluglike slowness. Even Marsden had difficulty calling them in line.

She urged her bay to gallop to the top of the lane, where she pulled the mare to a circling walk beneath a canopy of oak trees and thought about where she might ride next. Matching hedges lined either side of the road (a project coordinated years ago by her father and the viscount's sire), but Northwind could leap over them with ease, and she was as welcome to ride on Miles's property as her own. For the moment, though, she felt content to view her own home. At this distance it resembled a peaceful abode where civilized people dwelled. She sighed at the illusion.

A moment later she brightened. On the other side of the hedge, Miles was riding parallel to the road toward Oakwood. She doubted he had spotted her beneath the towering trees. With sudden mischief blooming, she spurred Northwind into a gallop that shadowed the viscount's route, although at a quarter mile's distance.

He could not fail to notice her from the corner of his vision, yet he turned not an eyelash in her direction. Nevertheless he leaned forward on his black, Damon, and the steed lengthened his stride, now angling toward the road instead of the stable.

She laughed delightedly. So it was to be that kind of game, was it? Bending toward Northwind's ears, she begged the mare to go faster. As the bay pressed harder, Damon accordingly stretched his legs. The viscount, to all appearances ignorant of her presence, was now as close to the hedge as she.

Determined to play the game according to his rules, she directed her vision straight ahead. She could not, however, stop her grin.

With horses puffing, they galloped on silently side by side with the hedge between them, until Oakwood Castle and Misthaven lay far behind. She passed an oxen-drawn cart filled with hay, then a laborer who shouted angrily and dashed to the opposite side of the road when she crested a hill.

"You'd best slow down," Miles shouted, yielding to speech at last. "Pity your countrymen if not your horse."

"Northwind needs no pity; she always enjoys besting Damon!" she threw back.

"If you have no mercy for her, then I shall have to," he called, pulling on his reins until Damon settled into a canter.

"Call it mercy if you will. I'm not one to crow at winning, nor is Northwind."

Smiling brilliantly as she slowed, Roslyn chanced a look at the viscount. Her heart constricted at the sight of his tumbled hair, flushed cheeks, and sparkling eyes.

"If you want a true race, come over to the green where you won't murder your neighbors," he said.

For an instant she considered it, but she felt too strangely, as if her insides were knotting into bows. "Some other day, perhaps. Damon's mouth is foaming; I don't want you to ruin him."

After a quick look of concern, Miles said, "You little liar, I should—" Seeing she had pulled her mare to a stop, he caught the expression in her eyes and halted his own steed.

She knew she should smile or make a jest to lighten the moment, but she could only gaze at him with all the solemnity and longing she felt. When the merriment faded from his face, she knew she must break the silence.

"You should . . . what?"

"Pardon?"

"You called me a liar and said you should . . ." She paused expectantly, then felt her heart accelerate as he continued to stare at her lips. "I think you wanted . . . revenge of some kind."

"How beastly of me," he murmured.

"*I* thought so." Her smile returned.

"You misunderstood," he said, recovering. "I was merely going to suggest that I accompany you home."

She fought disappointment, knowing she was wrong to feel it. "How kind you are." She turned

Northwind's head, then paused as Miles jumped Damon over the hedge.

"How is your mother today?" she asked as they ambled toward home. For once Miles appeared to be in no more hurry than she was.

"Very well, thank you. This morning she began making new altar cloths for chapel."

"How nice," Roslyn commented, sinking inside. Why didn't *she* ever think of such worthy projects? Every Sunday she attended the same chapel, and had even noticed how frayed the tapestries were growing. It had never occurred to her to do something about it herself. She was selfish, utterly selfish, just as Miles believed.

They moved onward in silence for a length of time. Northwind, still excited from the run, tossed her head and pranced, and it was only with difficulty that Roslyn held her under control.

"Roslyn—" the viscount began suddenly.

At the same time, she said, "Miles—"

"Go ahead," he said.

"No, you."

She could not find the words to express her heart. They were topping the final rise to Misthaven, and it was with relief that Roslyn noted a weatherworn coach in the drive of her home, a confusion of luggage and crates gathered round it with many more piled atop.

As the coachman tossed a small box with holes cut in the side to the butler, Roslyn heard an unpleasant voice screech, "Careful of my cats!"

"Cats?" Roslyn whispered, shivering with distaste.

"One of your houseguests, I presume?" Miles asked. Roslyn frowned at his tone of amused superiority. "She sounds charming. I can't wait to meet her."

Although the conveyance hid her from view, Roslyn had immediately recognized Harriet Pollehn's scratchy voice. It seemed her guest had arrived a day early. Fighting dismay that Harriet should be first, for she was the least favorite of Roslyn's circle, she prodded Northwind forward while putting a hospitable expression on her face. She wished Miles would go home, but he followed her—hoping for disaster, she was certain. As she circled the coach, however, she forgot all resentment when she saw Colleen Sheridan had traveled with Harriet. With a glad cry of greeting, she slipped from the saddle and welcomed her friends. When Miles dismounted and approached them, she recollected herself and performed introductions.

"Good, a lord," pronounced Harriet. "Tell these simpletons to have a care with my animals. Perhaps they will listen to you."

"It will be my pleasure," Miles said with a bow. Turning to Marsden, he said, "Here, men. Have a care with those beasts, will you?"

"Yes, milord," Marsden intoned, pausing, then resumed stacking one hissing and spitting cat above the other.

Roslyn stifled a horrified giggle. Even if Harriet did not resemble a dried twig—surely she'd had more flesh on her bones at the Academy!—she had lost all chances with the viscount before she began. He detested being used in such a fashion.

There was greater hope for Colleen. She looked well, although in the intervening years her figure had grown round—not unpleasantly so, Roslyn thought loyally. Her smooth skin and flushed cheeks glowed with health, and her midnight hair was thick and beautiful beneath a blue bonnet that matched her modish carriage dress. Even better, she cast frequent glances at the viscount beneath her lashes, proving her interest.

"It's nice to see neighbors riding together," she said. "Does your wife not enjoy the sport, Lord Beaumont?"

"I fear I am unwed, Miss Sheridan," the viscount said.

"La, but I find that hard to believe," Colleen said, her gaze traveling slowly up and down the length of him.

"Yet you must," he returned.

Colleen's laugh was so sudden and sharp that even Roslyn jumped in surprise. She had forgotten how *loud* Colleen could be, although her amusement was as infectious as always.

"What a quizzer you are!" Colleen moved closer to him. "You must turn the head of every girl in the village!"

"I've noticed a few turning away, yes."

Gales of laughter as Colleen rested her hand on the viscount's sleeve. "Modest, too! Roslyn, you never said what a prize you were keeping tucked away in your little village."

Her smile feeling strained, Roslyn began, "I
haven't—"

"You were surprised that we came together,
weren't you?" Harriet said, pushing her way between them to stand closer to her baggage. She
wore a straw bonnet pushed back carelessly on
her head, as though she'd been caught in a strong
wind, or had begun to remove the hat and then
forgotten it. "Traveling together was a measure
of economy. Two can ride more cheaply than one,
if they're going in the same direction."

"Harriet's journey took her directly through
Ipswich, and I met her in the village rather than
inconvenience her," Colleen said, her sardonic
glance telling Roslyn her feelings on the matter.
"Traveling to my home would have added three
miles to her trip."

"Time is not to be wasted," Harriet said. Wisps
of dun-colored hair trailed from its pins to frame
a face remarkable only for its intensity. "Not when
important scientific studies are being conducted."

Roslyn remembered Harriet as a serious girl,
but not one who, in less than five minutes, pro-
duced such waves of missionary zeal. Her curiosity
had only an instant to bloom when Mr. Andrews,
with a troubled glance at the growing pile of va-
lises and crates, exited from his home and descended the shallow stairs to greet the visitors.
Roslyn, knowing his true feelings concerning
company (particularly the feminine kind), felt
proud of how he exerted himself to be affable
until a sudden, piercing howl brought their con-

versation to a stop and drew all eyes to the crate nearest the door.

"Someone has brought cats, Roslyn," Thurmond Andrews said. *"Cats."*

"I did," Harriet said. "I hope you don't mind. My studies in animal behavior couldn't be interrupted, not when I'm so close."

"So close to what?" asked Mr. Andrews with a scowl. "A zoo?"

Oblivious to his displeasure and Colleen's giggles, Harriet said, "I've been observing how felines react to certain conditions in order to train them."

"Train a cat?" inquired the viscount.

"Impossible!" cried Mr. Andrews.

"Why would you want to train a cat?" Roslyn couldn't help asking. She shared her father's dislike for felines.

Colleen shook her head warningly. "Don't ask her that!"

Harriet's expression became more eager. "Because what can be done with animals might be useful with humans."

"Useful with—!" Mr. Andrews broke off as if beyond his endurance. With a telling look at his daughter, he said, "I leave your friends to you." To Marsden he added, "You can put the animals in the stable."

"Oh!" cried Harriet. "The stable? Oh, dear!"

With her father's eyes heavy upon her, Roslyn whispered, "Father has never allowed animals in the house."

"Then I shall have to stay in the stable, too."

"Harriet, you can't mean that."

"I mustn't leave them now, not when they're beginning to respond in reliable ways to my directions." With her chin trembling, Harriet added, "You would be surprised at what Three can do already."

Roslyn cast a look of appeal at her father. Waving his hand in a gesture of disgust, he walked to the door and said, "Put them in her room, Marsden, but I'd better not see hide nor paw of those furballs anywhere else in my house!"

Harriet clasped her hands and beamed. "They will be good, Mr. Andrews. You may depend upon it!"

Roslyn sent her father a grateful look, then felt the viscount's eyes resting on her. "This promises to be an entertaining visit," he said. "Unfortunately, I've just remembered that I have some business to take care of in London and need to be gone for a few days, perhaps a week or two."

Roslyn's heart thudded within her chest. "No, you cannot," she commanded.

"No, no!" Colleen chimed. "I shall take personal offense if you dash away so soon after meeting me! You wouldn't want to make me think so poorly of myself, would you, Lord Beaumont?"

"You promised," Roslyn said, holding her breath as Colleen gave him a long, pleading look.

He moved his glance from hers to Roslyn's. "Perhaps I can postpone the trip for a while," he said reluctantly, and allowed himself to be led into the house.

Roslyn breathed a sigh of relief. He would not,

could not escape her carefully prepared net, no matter how much he might wish to do so, no matter how cleverly he might try.

Four

"If only you could have seen Roslyn as she was at Montrose Academy," Victoria Pendergrass said on the following afternoon in tones that reminded Roslyn of a mother speaking indulgently of her errant child. "Such a troublemaker she was!"

"Indeed?" Jonathan asked, his eyes warm upon Roslyn. "I find that hard to believe."

"Do you?" Miles asked. He stood apart from them at the fireplace as though reluctant to join the group. "I don't."

Roslyn smiled thinly. She and her guests were taking tea in the parlor. Victoria had arrived late that morning, shortly before Jonathan and his brother Ned came to take up temporary residence at Misthaven. Gregory Burnsmith, the solicitor, had come with them, having been enlisted by the brothers to help round out the numbers. Her father, frowning at a magazine in his lap, sat in a chair near the window.

"I never wanted to attend Montrose," explained Roslyn, who was not enjoying the house party as much as she had hoped. Miles had not shown a glimmer of interest in her friends, only tolerance; and if truth be told, she was finding them all less amusing than she remembered. Colleen's sense of humor had acquired a desperate, shrill edge. Harriet's solemnity had taken a macabre turn with her obsession with her cats, and the young lady tried one's patience with her endless questions and serious pronouncements. Victoria still spoke with an innocent vapidity, yet seemed more *calculating* than Roslyn recalled.

"Don't sing that old song again," said Mr. Andrews. "Every girl needs her training in deportment and such."

"But Roslyn refused to learn accomplishments," Victoria said with a smile. She wore a pale muslin gown with a rounded neckline that displayed her admirable figure to advantage. "How the Misses Montrose despaired of her lack of motivation!"

"I admit I never saw the purpose of decorative box-making or bird-painting," said Roslyn, wondering what Victoria hoped to accomplish with this conversation. Did she think disparaging her hostess would make herself more appealing? She reminded Roslyn more and more of a matron who saw herself above the follies of youth. "But I did enjoy geography."

"You never liked embroidery. I remember that," Colleen said, giving her cloth and needle a little shake. After a second's hesitation, she held up her work. "Have I shown you my latest project? Adam and Eve in the Garden."

Roslyn blushed to the roots of her hair.

Stretched within the confines of an embroidery hoop, a seductive Eve was bestowing an apple upon her mate. No modest leaves or flowers twined to hide the charms of either figure.

"Oh, my," Victoria said, flicking open her fan and fluttering it in front of her face. "Really, Colleen."

"Very artistic," Harriet said, bending closer. "Don't be missish, Vicky. You'd think nothing if Michelangelo had done this. Needlework is one of the only ways females can express themselves creatively in our society."

Colleen laughed. "You make it sound as if I'm trying to put myself forward into the world of gentlemen, but I assure you I have no such plans. I simply enjoy embroidery."

"You have a talent for it," Miles said.

"Thank you, Lord Beaumont," she said, giving him a sizzling look that irritated Roslyn to an unreasonable degree. "I plan to do the entire Bible. I can hardly wait for *The Song of Solomon.*"

"Neither can I," Miles commented. "You must sew faster."

"At least you learned how to do something," grumbled Mr. Andrews over Colleen's howls of laughter. He had not been able to see the work from his angle.

"Don't be too harsh on your daughter," Victoria said with a compassionate smile. "She certainly learned leadership skills."

"Always had those," returned Mr. Andrews.

Between giggles, Colleen said, "La, but she was always leading us astray, weren't you, Roslyn?"

"My goodness, yes!" Victoria said. "Roslyn, do you remember the day you persuaded us to sneak away to Drury Lane to see *The Merry Mourners?*"

"What's this?" asked Jonathan with an uncertain smile.

"Yes, and we were almost murdered!" declared Harriet.

"We were not." Roslyn scowled. "That happened days later. A man rose from the pit and shot at one of the actresses."

"Killed her, did he?" Gregory inquired.

Roslyn gave the brown-haired solicitor a momentary stare. "No, she wasn't harmed at all."

"But she could easily have been," Victoria assured him. "As could the audience. It was not a place for young ladies, but we never could tell Roslyn *no.*"

"Why have I never heard this tale?" demanded Mr. Andrews.

To Roslyn's surprise, Victoria rushed to her father's side, bent over him, and seized his hand. "Please don't think badly of her, Mr. Andrews," she entreated. "She only meant the outing for amusement, and truly her reputation grew to lofty heights because of it. Roslyn was greatly loved at Montrose."

"Glad to hear it," he said gruffly, his glance flickering uncomfortably from Victoria to his daughter.

"I shouldn't have said anything," Victoria went on, staring earnestly into the older gentleman's eyes.

On that we can agree, Roslyn told her silently.

Victoria slowly withdrew her hand and folded her fingers together in a demure gesture. "It would devastate me to know I've worried you, even for an instant, after you've been so gracious to offer your hospitality to all of us."

"Ah, well." His glance dipped to Victoria's decolletage, then lifted guiltily. "No harm done."

"That's well, then." Victoria dimpled, pressed his hand a final time, and returned with evident reluctance to the settle. "You always were kind to us. I remember that from your visits to Montrose and from when I visited here once during the Christmas holidays. You probably don't recall my stay; I was such a child in those days."

Mr. Andrews declared he did remember her. While Roslyn's brows drifted downward, a sudden clatter of hooves sounded outside, drawing her attention to the window. Her father lifted the draperies to peer outward.

"Someone has come," he said. "A lad on horseback—no, a woman by all the stars—she's just removed her hat!"

"Perhaps it's Esther," Roslyn said gladly, too hopeful to wonder at her father's cryptic words. She hastened from the room in time to stand behind Marsden as he opened the front door. To her great pleasure, she saw her guest was indeed Esther Cummings, who was slowly mounting the steps. Rushing forward to embrace her, Roslyn could not help glancing downward from Esther's delicate, pinched face to her legs, which were encased in leather breeches.

"Esther?" she said, a world of inquiry in her tone.

"Quick, hide my horse," Esther said breathlessly. "Perhaps a servant could remove my bags, and I'll change into something more appropriate before anyone sees me."

Roslyn had not the heart to tell her it was too late for that. She instructed the butler to gather her guest's bags from the beast, then swept Esther toward the door.

"You look exhausted!" she said, leading her into the hall, where she was dismayed to see most of her guests had gathered in curiosity. "I'm amazed that you rode all this way."

Esther blanched when she saw the crowd. "It was necessary," she said softly to Roslyn. Forcing strength into her voice, she addressed the others. "Please forgive—my appearance, I—dressed as a lad for safety—perhaps you can understand—a woman on horseback alone is not wise, I—"

Roslyn hardly heard her; her eyes were upon Miles, who was approaching them rapidly. Just as Esther's voice trailed away, her knees buckling, Miles lifted the young woman into his arms with no more effort than he would a child.

After the viscount placed Miss Cummings on the divan in one of the guest bedrooms, Roslyn rang for a maid to bring water. Miles was relieved when she banned her friends from the room, but Miss Pendergrass insisted on joining them. She seemed the domineering sort.

Thurmond Andrews was pacing back and forth and casting nervous glances at the figure on the divan. "Should I send for the physician?"

"I think we should give her a moment," Roslyn said, continuing to pat her friend's hands. "She may only be overtired. I need water and towels. Where *is* Hetta?"

"Probably lying on a chaise longue eating chocolates," barked Thurmond.

"I shall see to it," Miss Pendergrass said, moving officiously to the door.

Roslyn lifted worried eyes to Miles. "I can't imagine the story behind this. Esther was always the most conventional one of us."

"I'm glad to know one of you fits that designation," he couldn't resist saying.

"How you can jest at a time like this?" Roslyn reproved him as she smoothed a lock of hair from Miss Cummings's forehead.

Outside the half-opened door came the sound of loudly clapping hands. "Butler! You there!" Miles recognized Miss Pendergrass's dulcet tones now crisped to command. "We need water and towels at once!"

Within moments Marsden appeared carrying the required items, with Miss Pendergrass following. Roslyn moistened a cloth and rested it on the invalid's forehead. Seconds later, the girl's lashes fluttered open.

"What—where—"

"Easy, my dear," Roslyn soothed. Miles had never heard her sound so motherly, and looked at her in surprise. "You're in a bedroom at Misthaven. Everything is all right."

The young woman's eyes widened. Taking in Thurmond and Miles, she tried to sit up, her cheeks flushing. When she faltered, Miles hurried to assist her. She looked fragile as a waif and made him feel instantly protective.

"I—I had hoped no one would see me like this," she whispered.

"Maybe you should lie back down," Miss Pendergrass urged. "Don't strain yourself, Esther."

The girl—she was so tiny, he could not think of her as a woman—shook her head. "No, I—may I—water, please?"

Roslyn poured a glass, and Miss Cummings gulped it down. "That's much better, thank you." The girl's eyes roamed between Thurmond and Miles. Roslyn quickly introduced them, an action that made the invalid seem even more uncomfortable. "You must think I'm the oddest creature," she said, her voice still weak. "I do beg pardon for appearing dressed in this manner."

"Don't worry an instant about it," Miss Pendergrass said, sounding for all the world like a hostess. Roslyn heard her tone, too, and frowned, making Miles want to laugh. "We're only glad you are safe."

Roslyn's gaze moved slowly from Miss Pendergrass to the invalid. "Are you hungry, dear?"

When the girl admitted she had not eaten since yesterday, Miss Pendergrass rose. "I'll fetch you something from the kitchen myself. The servants are a trifle slow here."

"You've noticed that, have you?" Thurmond grumbled.

Miss Pendergrass sent him a gracious smile. "They only want a firmer hand, sir. Perhaps I can speak with them."

"*I* shall speak to them later," Roslyn said emphatically. "I wouldn't dream of imposing upon a guest in such a manner."

"Certainly, Roslyn." Miss Pendergrass lowered her eyes. "Whatever pleases you, although I wouldn't have minded in the least."

"You say whatever you want, young lady," Thurmond said. "It couldn't hurt.".

Roslyn's eyes shot daggers at her father. When Miss Pendergrass exited, Thurmond huffed, "Well, Marsden never moved so fast for us as when *she* summoned him, did he?"

Miles waited with interest to see how Roslyn would respond to this, but Miss Cummings drew their attention as she asked if her horse had been hidden away.

"Yes, your beast is in the stables as you asked," Roslyn replied.

The girl's large, golden eyes turned downward. "I know you find the request peculiar. I should explain—and apologize—to you." She glanced at Miles. "And to all of your guests."

"You don't have to apologize for anything," Roslyn said.

"But I must. First I'd like to freshen up, if I may."

Roslyn assured her they awaited her pleasure and urged the gentlemen to exit.

Miles spent the next hour enduring Miss Sheridan's flirtations in the parlor, although he had to admit he was not the only object of her attentions. Only Miss Pollehn was ignored, a fact that did not seem to disturb her. She had a notebook in her lap into which she occasionally wrote. The rest of her time she appeared to be observing the others in the room. He found it deuced disconcerting.

In an attempt to bring the young woman into the circle—in truth, he felt sorry for her; she was plain as a fence post—Miles asked, "What is that you're writing there, a journal?"

She turned her head to the side, reminding him of a bird with her tiny nose and eyes and mouth. "Can't tell you. It might destroy the validity of my experiment."

Miles was saved the necessity of forming an answer by the astonishing entry of Miss Cummings. She wore a blue plaid day dress with long sleeves edged in lace. Her brown locks had been arranged into a chignon with wispy curls framing perfect features. Trusting, beautiful eyes gazed from one guest to the other as she paused beneath the arched doorway.

Miles, scarcely registering that Roslyn and Miss Pendergrass flanked her protectively, stood, as did the other gentlemen. Within seconds the young lady had been ensconced in the most comfortable chair in the parlor with an ottoman pulled to her feet.

"You will spoil me," she protested, her smile so genuine that Miles felt unaccountably warmed. When Jonathan Leffew brought a pillow for her back, she added, "Truly, I don't deserve such attention."

"And why not?" Jonathan said. "You've traveled a long way on horseback. Roslyn told me you live in Essex. Please don't say you've ridden so far . . . and alone."

She dipped her head. "I admit it was foolish. That's why I dressed as a lad, so that my journey would be safer."

"Why go alone at all?" Miss Pollehn asked, baldly voicing the question uppermost in the viscount's own mind, and, he suspected, in everyone else's.

The young lady's cheeks reddened. "I fear there were no funds to hire a coach."

"But your parents own a carriage. I remember you arriving at the Academy in it."

Miss Cummings blinked. "We don't—we lost—"

"Pockets to let," Miss Pollehn stated with a sage nod. "You've fallen on hard times, haven't you?"

"Yes," admitted Miss Cummings. Miles felt compassion at the girl's plight and wished the spinster with the crow's voice would leave her alone.

Jonathan's spine stiffened. "I don't think we should press the young lady any further."

"Nor do I," said his brother Ned, surprising everyone, for he was notoriously shy and seldom spoke. Miss Cummings appeared to spawn gallantry in all of their hearts, Miles reflected. An interesting trait.

Roslyn's father narrowed his eyes. "Do you

mean to say your parents allowed you to ride half-way across England unattended?"

The young lady's head dipped further, reminding Miles of a lamb awaiting slaughter. "No, sir," she whispered.

"Please say they know you're here!" exclaimed the older man.

"They do not," the girl said, blinking back tears.

"By all the stars!" Thurmond bellowed. "Marsden! Fetch pen and ink!"

"Please, sir," entreated Miss Cummings, one hand outstretched. "If you will allow me to explain . . ."

"Another moment will do no harm," Jonathan declared, and leaned toward the young lady. "Proceed, Miss Cummings, if you wish. You are among friends."

She inhaled deeply. "It all began two years ago when my father discovered his steward had mismanaged our estate and stolen funds. We were on the brink of ruin."

Roslyn's gaze, heavy with sympathy, met the viscount's for an instant. Miles understood her message, that she was in a similar situation. What would she think, he wondered, if she knew the truth about *him*? Would she look at him with sympathy or scorn?

Miss Cummings moistened her lips. "The only solution appeared to be a suitable marriage. As I am the oldest, my father soon betrothed me to a—a wealthy gentleman in our shire."

"Without consulting *you*?" Miss Sheridan asked

in tones of horrified delight. "Have you run away?"

After a brief struggle, the young lady said, "Yes, Papa did not consult me. And yes, I *have* run away. At least for a time. When Roslyn's invitation arrived, I couldn't resist a last opportunity for freedom. I don't know what I was thinking. I know I'll have to write my parents so they won't worry about me, and then I shall probably have to return home straightaway. But you see, my entire life has been decided for me." She turned glimmering eyes of appeal to them. "Can you understand how that feels? To have your future laid out before you as a book already written and not be able to exercise choice in the matter?"

"Yes," Miles said before he could stop himself. Hastily he added, "Often performing one's duty must take precedence over one's own desires."

"How stiff you sound!" Roslyn scolded.

Miss Cummings winced. "He's correct, of course. It's only that . . ."

"You don't like your intended," Miss Sheridan supplied eagerly. "He's fat, is he? Bald? Does he wash?"

"He's quite fine looking, actually," the girl said. "And tall with golden hair."

"And rich as well?" Miss Sheridan said with a disbelieving laugh. "What more could you want? Does he have all his teeth?"

"It's just that—I can't—" She looked from one to the other of them. "I shouldn't say more."

"I daresay not," Miss Sheridan said. "Bite your tongue for being ungrateful. Nothing like that will ever happen to me, but if it did, you wouldn't find me running from my fate. My father isn't wealthy, but he has sufficient to want his daughters about him forever."

"Miss Cummings is tired," Jonathan said. "We should allow her to rest before dinner."

"I agree," Miles said immediately, and offered his escort to her room, wondering if Jonathan had seen what he had, the look of terror in her eyes.

Five

Roslyn was putting the finishing touches on her hair that evening when a knock sounded at her bedroom door. Hetta entered, her face twisted in an ugly emotion.

"I never stole anything in my life!" she announced.

Before the young lady could respond, Victoria followed her into the room. "I didn't accuse her, Roslyn. She was helping me dress when I simply commented that my garnet pendant was missing—"

"She was helping you dress?" Roslyn asked, registering only part of her discourse. By what witchery had Victoria convinced Hetta to work?

"I didn't take it," the maid said.

"Did I hear something about missing jewelry?" Harriet inquired, pushing open the sitting room door. "My cat brooch with the ruby eyes is gone. What do you think it means?"

Roslyn turned to her own jewelry box. Everything appeared in order, except— "Where is my mother's opal ring?" she cried, facing Hetta reflexively.

Fists on hips, the servant glared back. "Sixteen years I've worked here and never once have I been accused of such. I won't have it!"

"Calm down, woman," Victoria said in firm tones. "No one is accusing you. Are there new servants on the premises, Roslyn?"

"No," she said, struggling to hide her resentment of Victoria's commanding manner. Much more of this and Roslyn would feel like a guest in her own home. But she was being petty; the important thing was her mother's ring and the other jewelry. "Perhaps I should order a search of the servants' quarters just in case."

"You won't win friends doing that," Hetta warned.

"Roslyn isn't looking for friends; she's looking for stolen goods," Victoria said.

Roslyn glanced from Victoria to Harriet. "Is there any chance you forgot to bring the pieces?"

"None," Harriet said. "I was wearing my cat pin when I arrived. And just last night Vicky showed me her garnet and her diamonds."

"Someone took the garnet and not the diamonds?" Roslyn asked incredulously.

"Maybe they didn't have time," Victoria said.

"Do you store them together?" When Victoria admitted she did, Roslyn said, "Then why would a thief have time to steal one stone and not another? And look—only my mother's ring has been taken. Harriet, are you missing anything else?"

"Only the brooch."

"None of this makes sense," said Roslyn.

"What will you do?" Harriet asked, her expression so inquisitive that Roslyn felt uneasy.

"Have Marsden search the servants' rooms," she ordered Hetta finally, feeling wrong but not knowing what else to order.

"They won't like it," said Hetta.

"And I don't like missing my garnet," Victoria said with a forbidding look. "My Aunt Alicia gave it to me on my eighteenth birthday and it means much to me."

Later, when the guests gathered around the long table in the dining room for a dinner of roast pork, baked apples, and vegetables, the missing jewelry naturally became the subject of conversation. Esther mentioned not being able to find the locket that held her parents' miniatures, although she admitted the possibility that she had not brought it at all, so distraught had she been when she stole away. Alarmed, Colleen left the table, and returned a few moments later to report her pearl choker was gone.

The thefts spurred everyone into conversation, and the group was lively in spite of slow service and sullen looks from the maids. Word of the room searches had spread, Roslyn imagined. Nevertheless, when the gentlemen joined them after port in the parlor, she had to admit her guests were fully as convivial as she had hoped. She ordered Marsden to bring in tables and cards, and several groups formed. Roslyn herself didn't want to play.

Feeling a headache coming on, she opened the French doors wide to admit the sweet night air, then walked onto the balcony and braced her forearms on the stone railing. The gathering was a success, she supposed, in spite of the thefts and the unexpected behavior of her friends. All of them appeared to have changed—even Esther, who remained as sweet as always but who would never have been caught in boy's clothing back in their school days. She wondered if all of them truly had changed, or if her *perceptions* of them had altered with maturity.

But why worry about such issues when she could not understand her own feelings? The purpose of the party was to find a match for Miles, but excepting Esther, he showed all the young ladies the same regard. And every time he fetched something for her dear friend or spoke to her solicitously, Roslyn felt a stab of jealousy that dismayed her for its intensity. And the worst of it was, Esther was betrothed and therefore presented no real threat to his affections. Was anyone in the world more foolish than herself?

"Tired of playing hostess already?" Miles asked from the doorway.

"Of course not." Roslyn was so deep in misery that, aside from a bittersweet thumping of her heart when he joined her at the rail, she scarcely reacted. "I thought you were playing whist."

"Miss Sheridan wanted a place at table. When she asked for Ned's chair, I gave her mine."

She couldn't help smiling at this. "And thus defeated her purpose in wanting to play, I'm certain."

"Are you trying to flatter me, Miss Andrews?"

Her smile widened. He was always able to pull her from a mood with his banter. Such an actor he was, sounding solemn but seldom meaning a word he said. No wonder the villagers thought him stiff, for they took him seriously. No one knew him as she did. No one understood how adorably amusing he could be. The thought tugged her downward again.

"You can't have missed Colleen's preference for you," she said.

"Actually, she seems to have an eye for any gentleman willing to speak with her."

"Please don't judge her harshly. Colleen will make someone a wonderful wife."

"As you say."

"You could do a lot worse," she said, then swiftly amended, "That is, any gentleman could." She wanted to shake herself for nearly revealing her plot.

He didn't appear to notice her slip. His eyes clouding with thoughts, he said, "I am concerned about one of your guests."

"Oh?" Her pulse began to race. He didn't have to say the name of the guest; she knew it instinctively.

"Miss Cummings," he said.

"I see." Turning her profile to him, she said bravely, "She's very lovely, isn't she?"

"Very—"

"And she has a kind disposition. It's genuine, too; there's nothing of fakery about Esther; she's been like that since I've known her."

"I don't doubt it a moment; one senses that she—"

"But she *is* betrothed, Miles," she said, facing him with an earnest expression. She could not bear to see him hurt; it was best she stop things before his affections were further engaged. "She's committed to someone, even if it is unwillingly."

He stared at her then, and she imagined he could see to the very roots of her heart. She shivered at the intensity of his look. For one insane moment, she willed him to gather her in his arms. Even as she thought it, guilt bloomed.

"I know about commitments," he said softly. From inside the house came the sound of Colleen's raucous laughter echoed by several gentlemen. The tension broken, Miles turned abruptly and rested one hand on the rail. "That's why I'm worried about Esther. She seems afraid."

Roslyn couldn't like how his thoughts centered so much on Esther, so she stared at his hand. She could not resist touching it, but she made the gesture a reassuring squeeze before interlocking her fingers at her waist. She feared it looked a silly pose, but a necessary one.

"I imagine you're concerned because she seems unhappy with her father's choice," she said. "Many young ladies are at first, but later find themselves blissfully wed."

"Is that how it is with you?" he asked, speaking so softly that her gaze dropped to his lips. "A silly question. You're fond of Jonathan."

"Fond," she nodded, whispering, still watching his mouth.

"He will make you a fine husband," he said, leaning ever so slowly toward her.

"A . . . fine . . . husband," she breathed mindlessly, and closed her eyes, her heart in her throat.

She felt the sweet warmth of his breath, sensed the nearness of his lips. But the expected kiss never came. Disappointed beyond measure, she slowly opened her eyes. When she saw that Miles was frowning at something in the doorway, she turned with a guilty start.

"Harriet!" she cried, much louder than she'd intended.

"Hope I'm not interrupting," the young woman said, her small eyes darting back and forth between them. "Wondered where you were."

"Of course you're not interrupting!" Roslyn exclaimed. "I was just getting some fresh air, for pity's sake! As was Lord Beaumont!"

A stunned expression stole across Harriet's features, frightening Roslyn until the young woman blurted out, "My cats! You've reminded me that if I don't air them, they'll be too wild to sleep tonight and too drowsy to work tomorrow!" Without another word, she disappeared into the parlor.

Miles gave Roslyn an amused look. "It's good to know we serve a useful purpose in life," he said, leading her toward the parlor, making her smile in spite of the heaviness in her heart.

It was almost as though the past minutes had never happened.

* * *

Fool, fool, fool.

The words became the viscount's litany over the next two days as he did everything in his power to amend his actions on Friday evening. He could only hurt Roslyn by letting his true feelings slip into the open, and hurting her was the last thing he wished to do.

If only matters had been different. But one had to deal with reality as it was. At least he had the compensation of knowing Roslyn felt tenderly toward her betrothed. He would not stand in the way of her happiness. *Could* not. Had he been free to do as he pleased long ago, matters would not have fallen to this point. But life was like that sometimes. One had to adjust.

Therefore he turned his attentions to Esther Cummings. At every opportunity he tried to put himself at her service. He felt sorry for the chit. She had a gift of some sort that made him feel responsible for her. Evidently the other gentlemen felt the same, for often they competed to run errands or bring her refreshments, all for the reward of one of her smiles.

Thus he did not find an opportunity to question her alone until Sunday afternoon after chapel. The day was splendid, and several of the young people, Roslyn included, were playing a loud game of croquet in Misthaven's back garden. The rest of them watched at small tables scattered across the terrace. Esther was the last to exit from the house, and Miles made the most of his opportunity by leading her to his table.

They passed a few moments in pleasantries before the viscount directed the conversation in the direction he wished. Nodding toward Roslyn, he said, "She looks very happy, don't you think?"

This was perhaps not the most propitious moment for his question, for Roslyn was arguing with Miss Pendergrass over the legalities of her last stroke. But Esther must have taken his comment in the spirit it was given, for she said, "I hope she is. She *should* be. Jonathan—Mr. Leffew—is—is very kind."

"I'm sure he wouldn't mind your using his given name," he said with a smile, finding her shyness charming. "None of us do. A gathering of this intimacy and length makes such formality unnecessary, don't you think?"

"I suppose so, Lord Beaumont."

He peered beneath her bonnet with a teasing look. "I'm glad you agree, *Miss Cummings*."

She laughed. "Miles, I meant to say."

He nodded approvingly. "Very good, Esther."

Marsden appeared at their table carrying a tray of lemonade, and both accepted a drink. After draining half his glass, Miles said carefully, "I'd like to think all brides-to-be are as fortunate as Roslyn, but from what I gathered from your arrival, you aren't looking forward to your wedding."

He cursed himself when the light died from her eyes and her head lowered. She clasped her glass with both hands and stared into the liquid as if it contained the secrets of the ages. Impulsively, he surrounded her fingers with his own.

"Forgive me, Esther. I shouldn't pry into what isn't my concern."

"No, it isn't that," she rushed to say. "I—truly, I'd feel relieved to confide in someone. It's only that . . ."

A shadow fell across the table at the same time her eyes raised. Annoyed, Miles looked up to see Jonathan looming over them.

"I . . . hope I'm not intruding," he said.

"Of course you aren't," Esther said, the color rising to her cheeks as she withdrew her hands from the viscount's. "Would you care to join us?"

"Only if it's not an imposition." Jonathan's regretful eyes fell upon the viscount. "I wouldn't like to interrupt a private conversation."

Why did you, then? Miles wanted to say, but it would be as cruel as swatting a moth with a boulder.

"We were just now speaking of you and Roslyn and how happy your marriage promises to be," Esther said.

Jonathan's gaze sought and found Roslyn, who at this moment was watching their table with an intent expression. "I am a fortunate man."

You don't know how fortunate, Miles thought, his mood turning surly.

"Both of you are blessed in finding each other," Esther said. "I only wish . . ."

After a moment, Jonathan said in a gentle voice, "What is it you wish, my dear?"

"To know the kind of happiness you have," she said softly. "To be . . . unafraid."

The viscount's eyes met Jonathan's. "Do you mean to say you fear your betrothed?" Miles asked. He'd suspected something of this nature.

"Braxton has never threatened me," she said, "but there is something about him that disturbs me." She shook her head and frowned prettily. "Oh, it's probably as my mother says, only in my mind. Certainly he has many admirers. Papa declares the gods of fortune smiled upon our family when Braxton's notice fell upon me. But he has a harsh temper and little kindness." Her eyes turned glassy. "Do you know how dogs often chase a passing carriage? More than once I've seen Braxton deliberately run them over."

Miles guiltily recalled crushing a chicken beneath the wheels of his phaeton only last month, but he hadn't intended it. "A brute," he commiserated.

"Hardly the behavior of a gentleman," Jonathan agreed.

Her voice dropped so low that both gentlemen had to lean closer to hear. "I expect he will be very displeased with me for running away."

"Have you written your parents to tell them where you are?" Jonathan asked.

"Yes, upon my arrival, since Roslyn's father required it."

"Then I daresay we'll be hearing from him soon," Jonathan said, a thoughtful expression in his eyes.

"I fear so."

"Perhaps I can have a word with him," Jonathan added.

"We both will," pledged Miles, who longed to see happiness restored to the girl's eyes.

This appeared to agitate her. "I do thank you

for the sentiment," she said, "but I'm afraid you will only make him more angry. Braxton doesn't take kindly to advice."

That would depend on how the advice was given, thought Miles. He glanced upward. Roslyn was approaching them purposefully, her croquet mallet swinging from her fingers. Beneath a pink bonnet, her cheeks were flushed, and tendrils of chestnut hair had loosened to frame her face. Though her eyes sparkled, her mood was unreadable. To him she appeared inexpressibly lovely.

"You are all looking very serious," she said. "Is anything the matter?"

Miles commanded himself not to smile. Roslyn was not one to be left out of things and never had been. Before he could answer her, a feminine scream sounded from the house. He exchanged a glance of surprise with Roslyn and took to his feet. As he and the others were running toward the back entrance, the scullery maid flew through the door.

"Help!" she cried. "Monsters!"

Six

Roslyn pushed through the kitchen door seconds behind Miles and Jonathan. Gerta, the scullery maid, crowded beside her, chattering explanations too incomprehensible to be understood. When Roslyn saw several marauding felines on Cook's mixing table, however, all became clear. The cats were sniffing and padding across a sheet of dough while Cook shouted, waved her rolling pin, and slapped them off the table. As soon as one landed on the floor, another leaped up to take its place. Worse, the felines were growling, hissing, and at least two meowing at a screaming pitch.

Roslyn didn't know whether to laugh or cry. One thing was certain: the path of paw prints through what should have been tonight's pastry revolted her.

Miles and Jonathan immediately charged to action. Jonathan raised a hand to still the cook's outrage, then began to speak softly to the animals as he approached. Miles eyed him skeptically, grabbed a towel, threw it over the nearest cat, and tossed the writhing bundle out the door.

A scream sounded behind Roslyn, and seconds later Harriet burst into the kitchen. "Stop! You'll hurt my cats!"

"By all the stars, what's this!" exclaimed Roslyn's father, huffing through the door. "I knew those animals would be trouble. Into the stables with them!"

"But you don't understand," Harriet cried. "They're really being good! Only think, they were able to release themselves from their cages and open a closed door in order to find their way to the kitchen! Do you know how long it took me to train them to do that?"

Roslyn bit her lip to prevent herself from laughing at the wild expression in her father's eyes. As his mouth opened and closed in outrage, she willed him not to say the hundred-and-one retorts she knew were welling inside his mind. When he pointed commandingly at the door without speaking, she felt relieved nothing worse had transpired.

Miles winked at her as he walked past with a cat beneath each arm, each wrapped in a towel. At the table, Jonathan was trying to persuade the two remaining cats to come to him, but one deliberately turned and jumped to the floor while the other arched its back and bared its fangs.

"Come to me, Five," Harriet was saying in a broken voice. "Here, Five, before someone hurts you."

The cat skittered across Roslyn's shoes. Disgusted, she tried to herd it toward the door with one foot, but it leaped over her slipper gracefully.

At that moment, Esther entered and the cat raced for the freedom of an open door. With a delighted cry, she scooped the animal into her arms before it could escape. After stroking it briefly, she handed the cat to Harriet, then approached the table.

"No, Miss Cummings," Jonathan said, seeing her intentions. "This one will scratch you."

"It will not be the first time," she said with a smile, and pulled Cook's stool to the table. Sitting, she looked away from the cat and made a curious rolling noise with her tongue, making a sound very like a purr. Still ignoring the feline, she tapped her fingers in her lap. Seconds later, the cat cautiously lowered himself into her arms.

"Well done, Miss Cummings!" Jonathan praised.

From the doorway came the sound of lightly clapping hands. "Amazing," Miles commented.

Esther blushed. "You make too much of a small thing," she said. "I love cats; I think they sense that."

Roslyn looked from Miles to Jonathan and back again. Their eyes were alight with tenderness and admiration as they gazed at Esther. It was no wonder, she thought. No one would look at *her* like that, not so long as she cowered against the wall for fear a tiny defenseless animal might breathe upon her. And if they suspected she was feeling resentment toward Esther for simply being her usual dear self, no one would stomach her presence at all.

She was tired of being selfish, tired of being

herself. Starting at this moment, she would become another person entirely, someone everyone could respect.

She had already tried to pattern herself after the viscount's mother by treating Hetta with consideration, an inner voice warned, and failed miserably. But this time she would succeed. This time she would be completely different and cause Miles's—no, Jonathan's—eyes to glow for *her.*

The new Roslyn surfaced straightaway. When Victoria charged into the kitchen to instruct Cook on how to rescue dinner, Roslyn thanked her for her thoughtfulness. After a sudden spring shower drew them all indoors, she endured an hour's viewing of Colleen's sketches of former sweethearts without complaint, even though the bare chests of the gentlemen embarrassed her mightily. (How Colleen had persuaded them to pose so, she could not imagine, and to where had all these admirers flown? But those were questions of her old self, and she dismissed them as uncharitable.)

She even brought supper to Harriet, who had spent the afternoon in the stable with her cats. Harriet looked pitiable, Roslyn thought, with her eyes red from weeping and straw in her hair. The thin young woman set upon the cold chicken and cheese heartily enough, however.

"Come inside now," Roslyn said kindly to her guest, stifling an impulse to berate Harriet's silliness. "You surely can't stay in the stable all night. It's too damp, and you'll catch a chill."

Harriet expressed her willingness to do so, though she added, "I wanted to stay long enough to feel certain my cats are safe before leaving them. Perhaps another hour will do. They've gone through much disturbance today and are very high-strung."

Roslyn glanced at the array of sleeping cats and forced herself to nod. "Have you made sure they can't escape this time?"

"The groom doesn't think they'll try because of the horses," she said.

As if summoned, the tall figure of Roger Crim meandered down the stairs from his room to approach them. "I hope you'll go along with Miss Roslyn now, Miss Cummings. I'll take good care of your pets."

Harriet, wiping her fingers, did not look up at him. "They're not my pets, Mr. Crim," she said primly.

"Right, your experiment, then. They'll be safe with me, miss."

"Very good," she said, rising, and hurried toward the door. Roslyn blinked at her sudden change of heart, quickly stuffed the remains of supper into the basket, then ran after her guest. Harriet was halfway to the house before she caught up with her.

"What do you do when you're angry?" Harriet inquired, her eyes centered on the house.

Raise my voice at the person making me angry, Roslyn thought, but those were old ways of thinking. "Riding can be calming," she mused.

"I don't ride."

Roslyn gave her a direct look. "Harriet, I hope you're not vexed with my father for asking you to put the cats in the stable."

"I don't want to be an imposition," she said noncommittally. "I was thinking of leaving tomorrow."

"Oh, I wish you wouldn't!"

"Well . . . my experiment isn't done yet . . ."

Roslyn rolled her eyes; she couldn't prevent herself. Hoping Harriet hadn't seen it, she said, "There you are, then. You can't possibly leave until you've finished your experiment. Your cats would never forgive you."

When Harriet looked at her, then smiled grimly, Roslyn congratulated herself. She had successfully banked down her impulse to send Harriet and her beasts packing. Surely no hostess, no matter how gracious, could have outdone her.

Returning to the parlor, she even managed to smile with the socially correct measure of regret when Miles announced he was leaving before cards. She would rather have pleaded with him to stay—such a childish thought! Certainly it was acceptable to walk him to the door, however, and this she did.

"You're probably weary," she said in understanding tones as he awaited his hat and gloves from Marsden.

"Not in the least. Why, are you?"

"No," she admitted. At least not physically. Gritting her teeth through a constant grin was beginning to be tiresome, though.

"Then why should I be tired? I'm only three

years older than you, not *five* years older or even
nine. There's still life in me yet."

She chose to ignore this dig. "Then why are
you leaving?"

"Because I have an estate to run, Roslyn. I can't
spend every moment over here." He studied her
face a moment. "No need to look sullen. I'll be
back tomorrow."

"I don't look sullen!"

He gave a short laugh. "Whatever you say."
Growing serious, he added in a quiet voice, for
Marsden was approaching, "But talk to Esther,
won't you? She has grave problems with her fiancé
and could use a kind ear."

Esther, always Esther, Roslyn thought sourly. But
she told him in her sweetest voice that she would.

There was no opportunity to speak privately
with Esther until everyone retired for bed. After
waiting an interval, Roslyn knocked at her guest's
door. The young lady appeared surprised but
pleased to see her, and Roslyn entered her room
feeling shame. Here stood her dearest friend
from Montrose, her life was in shambles, and
Roslyn had spent three days feeling jealous of her.

Esther invited her to sit in the bedroom's rock-
ing chair while she climbed into bed and sat up-
right against the pillows, curling her legs beneath
her. Roslyn wasted no time in getting to the point.

"You've told me little about your betrothed. I'm
anxious to hear more about him."

"Oh. Did the gentlemen tell you what I said

this afternoon? I probably gave them the wrong impression. Sometimes I start talking and can't stop."

"I've never known you to do so. Miles only mentioned that you have some reservations about your fiancé. But perhaps I'm prying where I'm not wanted."

"Oh, no," Esther rushed to say. "Why do you think I took such a risk in coming here? I've wanted to speak to you from the beginning, but you seemed busy with everyone. I knew we'd have our chance, though."

Roslyn wilted under this assessment, her heart softening toward her friend by the moment as she listened in growing disturbance to Esther's story.

"But Esther," she said when the young lady paused, "have you not told your parents of your concerns?"

"They think I'm being oversensitive, and perhaps they're right. Yet I can't feel as my father does, that brutalizing animals is a young man's way of spending excess energy." While Roslyn agreed, Esther blinked rapidly. "There's worse. I haven't told anyone this, but . . . Braxton . . ."

"Go on," Roslyn urged.

"He . . . oh, this is so shameful. He . . . grabs me sometimes and kisses me."

Roslyn very nearly smiled, but stopped herself in time. "I don't see how he could help *that*. You're his betrothed, after all, and quite beautiful."

Esther made a face. "Thank you, but you're much better-looking than I, yet Jonathan doesn't grab *you* as a savage would and cover *your* face and neck with kisses, does he?"

"No," Roslyn said slowly, her eyes widening at the thought. "No, he has never kissed me."

"Then you understand me. Jonathan is a *true* gentleman."

"Yes," said Roslyn, rising and walking to the door numbly. "He is."

No one had ever *really* kissed her, not even Miles in their courting days, although there had been a few playful exchanges in childhood. Did that mean she was surrounded by true gentlemen, or was she simply undesirable? She might be the kind of woman who brought out feelings of kindness in a man, pity even, but no passion.

Dear God!

Esther slid from the bed and came toward Roslyn, her eyes looking fearful and full of purpose. "Look," she whispered, and swept up the sleeves of her nightgown.

Roslyn gasped when she saw the pattern of bruises on her friend's arms. "He did this?"

She nodded, and tears welled in her eyes. "I can't tell you how he frightens me."

Heart sinking, Roslyn embraced her. "Don't worry, Esther," she whispered. "Please don't cry, my dear. We'll think of something."

But no solutions presented themselves to Roslyn, even after a night of little sleep. By the time she arrived late in the small dining room the next morning, Jonathan, Ned, and Gregory had already left for a ride, and Harriet had gone to her cats in the stable. Miles had not yet arrived. These facts she learned while speaking sleepily to Victoria and Colleen, who were eating their breakfasts.

After staring without appetite at a platter of toast and stone-cold eggs on the sideboard, Roslyn poured a cup of tea, and was taking her place at the table when she heard heavy footsteps descending the stairs.

"By thunder, Roslyn!" her father exclaimed as he charged into the room. "Someone has stolen my pocket watch, the one your mother gave me!"

"Are you certain you haven't misplaced it, Father?" After the servants' quarters had been searched to no avail, Roslyn had hoped the matter of missing jewelry would be gradually forgotten, attributed to carelessness or forgetfulness on the part of the owners. It would save the discomfort of trying to find the culprit, a thing she didn't relish doing as it could cause even greater resentment among the servants.

"Of course I'm certain! I've placed that watch next to my comb for these past twelve years!"

"Well, don't be angry with me; *I* didn't take it," she said. "What do you suggest we do? The servants' rooms have been gone through already, and nothing was found."

At this juncture, Marsden entered the room, looking regal as a king with his straight spine and heavy lids. "Is anything required, sir?" he asked in icy tones.

He had heard every word, of course. Roslyn was

sending her father a troubled look when Victoria said, "Why should the thief be one of the servants?"

"You mean you think one of *us* could have taken the jewelry?" Colleen asked with a nervous laugh.

Victoria glanced from Marsden to Roslyn's father. "Since nothing was found when Roslyn commanded that the servants' belongings be searched—a rash act I'm sure she now regrets, but she can't be blamed for not being able to think of a better plan of action—then it seems to me we should cast a wider net. But what do *you* think, Mr. Andrews? I trust your judgment in all things."

She was looking very demure, Roslyn thought with a betrayed feeling. Victoria had been the first to complain when her pendant went missing, and now she was acting as though she didn't hold any responsibility for pressuring Roslyn to do something. What was she about, trying to insinuate herself with the servants? Whatever it was seemed to be working. Marsden's face had softened to the point where he appeared almost human.

"I'll not allow our guests' belongings to be searched," said Roslyn's father.

"Certainly not!" Victoria said immediately. "I hope you don't think I'd suggest such a thing." Glancing briefly at Marsden, she said, "My idea was more along the lines of enlisting the servants to help us."

"How's that?" Mr. Andrews asked. Roslyn, seeing how attentive and respectful were her father's eyes, gazed from him to Victoria and back again. If ever he regarded *her* opinion with such interest, she would die of shock.

"Why, by asking them to keep their eyes open as they go about their chores. Not that they would deliberately *search;* I don't mean *that*. But sometimes one can discover things simply by being alert. I've found your servants to be very intelligent, sir; a cut above what I'm used to seeing. I believe you may depend on them."

"It wouldn't hurt, I suppose," Mr. Andrews said.

"I shall tell the maids straightaway," Marsden said. "May I pour you fresh tea, Miss Pendergrass?"

Victoria smiled with charming restraint. "No, thank you, Marsden, but I'm certain Mr. Andrews would like one."

"Wouldn't mind a cup at all," said Roslyn's father, looking pleased.

Roslyn couldn't like where her thoughts were leading—that Victoria was trying to charm her father. She would have thought herself completely ridiculous had not Colleen sent her a telling look and smirked.

She was beginning to regret inviting her friends. She'd done so to find Miles a wife, but he was interested only in Esther, a fact that presented two unforeseen problems. First, Roslyn had not anticipated how much his being attracted to someone would hurt. Secondly, Esther was betrothed.

But only because her parents needed funds for

their estate, whispered a detestable voice in her mind. Miles was a viscount and owned a fine property. No parent alive could possibly object to him.

If Esther received permission from her father to beg off her unfortunate betrothal, then Miles would be free to pursue her. Given the temper of Braxton Ames, she would doubtless need a defender, which would spur the viscount's interest even more since he seemed so very *protective* these days.

Miles and Esther would make a perfect match. And for the next fifty years, on an almost daily basis, she would have the pleasure of seeing her two best friends enjoy married life together. And all the while, she and Jonathan would be growing older, smiling and nodding, smiling and nodding.

Helping Miles and Esther find happiness would certainly be the act of a selfless woman, she thought, utterly miserable.

"What's wrong, Roslyn?" Colleen asked. "You're staring into your cup like a Gypsy. Are you reading your future in the grounds?"

"Perhaps she simply wants another cup of tea," Victoria said with a nod to Marsden, who moved immediately to the sideboard.

"No, thank you," Roslyn said, rising. "I have errands to run and can't delay another minute."

"What errands?" her father asked doubtfully.

"Hetta told me that Lottie Greene is ill," Roslyn said. "I'm bringing her a basket of food and some liniment for her joints."

"You're doing *what?*" Mr. Andrews cried with

such amazement that Roslyn wanted to stamp her foot.

"What a lovely thing to do," Victoria said. "Would you like me to accompany you?"

"No! I mean, no, thank you." She flashed a smile to remove the sting, then hurried from the room.

It wasn't so much that she minded being with Vicky, for when gentlemen were not around, she seemed more like her old self. But Roslyn needed to be alone to do some serious thinking.

It was time to stop denying the truth.

The role of Cupid was never an easy one, especially when Cupid was in love with one of the targets of her arrows.

Seven

Miles delayed arriving at Misthaven for as long as he dared that morning, jumping Damon across the hedge shortly before noon. He didn't want to risk Roslyn's wrath by dawdling longer, but truth! He was tired of playing escort to her friends. Only Esther struck him as tolerable, but one could take a steady diet of sweets only so long.

Whatever possessed Roslyn to desire such a houseful of women he couldn't imagine, but a lady approaching her wedding must be granted a few insane wishes, he supposed. It was exquisite torture for him, though, to be in her company for such lengths and to know she didn't belong to him and never would.

He was nearing the stable when he saw Thurmond Andrews approaching from the house.

"Good timing," said the older man, coming to stand by Damon. "No, don't get off, lad; you can do me a favor by riding out to Lottie Greene's. Roslyn headed that way on foot a good two hours ago, and luncheon is about to be served. I'd appreciate your fetching her."

Miles said he'd be glad to do so, but as he

turned Damon's head to leave, Miss Pollehn ran from the stable. Hatless, her hair flying from its pins like clumps of straw, her eyes shining, she looked almost pretty with excitement.

"Please come into the stable, Mr. Andrews, Lord Beaumont," she begged. "You must see what my cats have learned to do!"

"No, no," said the older gentleman, backing away. "I've no liking for cats. Surprised you haven't noticed."

"I have, of course! That's why I want you to observe them, so that you'll understand how talented they are. Now, we've been working for some time on many of the tasks they do, but I've changed their routine to fit the greater dimensions of the stable. You will be amazed at how quickly they've adapted!"

"I never saw the like," Roger Crim said, ambling from the stable with more energy than Miles had ever seen him display. "You'll want to look, sir, milord. She's done miracles with them cats."

Harriet's cheeks glowed. "Please," she begged, glancing from one to the other.

Miles exchanged a look with Mr. Andrews and shrugged. Dismounting, he and the older man followed the girl and groom inside the stable.

Miles noticed nothing remarkable at first; the cats were lined in a row within their cages. The one she called Three, the black-and-white, glared with mean yellow eyes; the rest ignored him.

The viscount then noted that a course had been arranged down the middle of the stable. Bales of

hay were piled in varying levels of stacks, rather
like stairs.

Before he could wonder further, Miss Pollehn
opened the first two cages. A yellow tabby meandered forth while the gray sniffed suspiciously,
then leaped across the edge of the box as though
it were poison.

"Look at me," she commanded the animals.

Immediately, the gray crouched into a hunter's
pose and began to track a large, slow-moving spi-
der. The tabby planted himself on his haunches
and stared at the rafters, looking for all the world
like a tourist admiring a cathedral, the viscount
thought on a rising tide of humor.

In a distraught voice Miss Pollehn said to the
gentlemen, "You're making them restless."

"The feeling's mutual," Mr. Andrews said.

"Attention!" she snapped. Startled, all three
men stared obediently, but she was only talking
to the cats. Miles saw the felines did notice her
this time.

"Mice!" she said in a glad voice, and clapped
twice.

The gray moved first, leaping from one stack
to the other, climbing a knotted rope stretched
to the loft, leaping downward onto a pile of hay,
bounding to the end of the stable where she
pawed a bell into ringing, then racing back to
Miss Pollehn, who rewarded her with a morsel of
cheese. The yellow followed more slowly and
skipped a few of the tasks. The entire affair took
no longer than half a minute.

The young lady accepted the men's congratulations with pride, but the light died from her face when Mr. Andrews asked the purpose of the drill.

"Purpose? The purpose is to see if cats can be trained by repetition and reward. I think I've demonstrated that."

"But why? It's not as though they do anything useful."

"If animals can be taught to obey by my method, then people can be, too. Imagine the implications for child-raising!"

"What parent would wish his child to run through a stable and climb ropes like an idiot?" Mr. Andrews huffed.

Seeing wrath gathering in the girl's eyes, Miles said swiftly, "Have all of the cats learned the course?"

"All except Three. He's part of another experiment. I'm isolating him from all activities to see how adept he is at socializing when I release him in a few days."

Things didn't look too promising from the look of him, Miles thought, but he murmured non-committally and returned to Damon.

Lottie Greene's cottage was placed beyond a slight hill no more than a mile from the Andrews home. An elderly, fractious woman, Lottie had served as a housemaid for many years before being pensioned off. He couldn't imagine why Roslyn had decided to visit her.

He found the cottage in excellent repair but saw no sign of Roslyn. Dismounting, he knocked at the door. Disturbed when no one answered, he stated loudly that he intended to open the door, and did so.

"Can't a woman have a minute's peace?" complained Lottie Greene from her bed. The white-haired old lady raised herself on one elbow. "Lud, if it ain't the viscount. I *must* be dying if you've come to see me."

"No, Miss Lottie," he said, venturing a couple of paces inside the darkened room. "I was told Miss Andrews came to visit you, and I'm here to fetch her."

"She ain't home yet? I ran her off, I have to say. She comes swishing in here with a basket of food I can't eat because of these poor old gums, which she ought to know about as I ain't had teeth since she was a girl, so I told her to take it to somebody what wants it. Think I set her off a bit, 'cause she said she *would* give it to someone who's grateful, said it as tart as a green apple, and flounced off. You can tell *she* ain't never been sick a day in her life."

Miles had already backed himself to the threshold, and now he thanked Lottie and moved outside before she could say more.

The remaining cottages were spaced at intervals that allowed for good-sized gardens and privacy. Knowing the next two were empty, as the families had recently emigrated to Australia, he rode past them briskly. It was then he spotted Roslyn in the distance running toward him. Immediately, he urged Damon into a gallop.

When he saw that Roslyn was being chased by several dogs, he shouted at his black to go faster.

The animals were gaining on her; he felt her panic as if it were his own.

Why had she started running? he thought angrily. Didn't she know dogs never refused a hunt?

He had almost reached her when she tripped headlong. Without pausing, he rode past her and took his whip to the animals. Excited barks and snarls turned to yelps. Within seconds the beasts reversed direction and disappeared into a stand of trees near the road.

Leaping off Damon, he ran the short distance to Roslyn, who was rising to her feet from what he now saw was a puddle from yesterday's rain. Her blue gown was streaked with mud, and a smear of dirt marred her cheek and nose. She came toward him with such a look of woe that he couldn't resist taking her in his arms.

She seemed receptive at first, but then stiffened and pushed him away.

"Are you laughing at me?" she cried.

He lengthened his face and drew her to him again. "Of course I'm not laughing," he said, biting his lip fiercely. "I'm just relieved you're all right. You *are* all right, aren't you?"

"No, I'm not," she said into his waistcoat, her voice wobbling. "I've tried to be kind, kind as your mother is, but no one wants my kindness. Miss Lottie was horrible to me this morning, and then I went to the Ashworths, and they took the bread and jam but kept asking me if I was bringing the food because my father planned to throw them from their home—and when I said he wasn't, they didn't believe me! They were all scowling as I left, and the little ones were crying, and when they went inside their dogs came after me!"

The viscount made a sound in the back of his throat, then managed to murmur, "You poor dear," while stroking her hair. She had lost her bonnet somewhere; her pins had loosened, and lustrous strands were falling around her shoulders. He found himself growing distracted by the smoothness of her hair and wished fashion would allow her to wear it down all the time.

"Nothing like this ever happens to your mother," she wailed.

"N-ho," he said, then coughed. His lungs were going to burst with pent-up laughter. "But she's been doing this sort of thing for a l-hong time."

"It's as I told you at the ball. Playing Lady Bountiful is simply not for me. The servants have never treated me so badly as they do now. Everything I do for them causes ill feelings. If I act kindly toward one, the others become jealous. Now they won't listen to anyone except Victoria!"

"Oh, it can't be so bad as that," he said soothingly.

She pulled back and glared at him. "Well, it is! You've seen how they are with me."

"They're out of their routine with so many guests, that's all." He released her, then removed his handkerchief and dabbed her cheek. She accepted his ministrations by turning her face to the side, her expression solemn. "After your company is gone, things will return to normal."

"Do you think so?"

He was so preoccupied with her face that he didn't answer. When he had wiped the worst of the dirt away, he tugged her chin in his direction. The beautiful wide eyes staring into his were luminous with tears, and he no longer felt like laughing.

"Roslyn, why were you trying so hard to imitate my mother?"

For a moment he thought she wasn't going to answer, but she finally said, "Because she's such a good and kind woman and—and everyone admires her."

"But you're good and kind, too. Without doing all these other things."

"That's not what you said at the ball," she said. "You said that society expects ladies to act in a certain manner, to minister to the sick and poor, to spend their days doing good deeds in all kinds of weather, such as taking food and blankets to people whether they want them or not." As her voice increased in volume, she began to pace. "To knit and sew and make things no one will wear because they are too fine and not at all practical. To leave the larger issues, such as whether or not the roofs are dry or the cottages whitewashed, to one's father, or husband, even though they might never think to do such tasks on their own. To avoid arranging for periodic medical examinations, especially for the children. Most of all, *most of all*, to involve oneself in petty issues and not the ones that really matter!"

"I said all that?" he asked weakly. And then,

taking umbrage; "Are you implying my mother's work is trivial?"

She stared at him, then appeared to deflate. "Of course not. It's only that I cannot be like her."

"No one expects you to be. You're delightful just as you are."

A joyful spark lit her eyes, but she quickly veiled it with her lashes. "That's not what you said at the ball," she repeated.

"Oh, never mind what I said at the deuced ball." He had never meant it anyway, had only spoken to distract her from thoughts of a love that was impossible. And now he was in a worse place than before, a lonely stretch of road and pasture with no one to see, with the blood crying in his veins to grab her and never let go. "Why should you care what I think, anyway?" he added rashly, angry at his helplessness to decide his own fate.

She gave him a direct look and said softly, "You know why."

As he gazed into her eyes, he was conscious of time passing, of insects moving through the grass, of a faint breeze whispering past his face, of opportunities rising and dying while he remained silent, still as a mindless, cold statue. But what could he say? He thought of brushing off the moment with; *Yes, I know why—because we've been friends for so long and you value my opinion.* But she deserved more than that, especially after that night when he'd very nearly kissed her in his madness.

Instead of mouthing untruths, he let the moment pass without saying anything. Roslyn interpreted his silence in her own way, bringing him low when she said quietly, "I'd better go home. They'll be expecting me."

He seized upon it. "Yes, your father sent me after you."

A moment later he was upon Damon with Roslyn settled in front, though she protested about mussing his clothes. He held his steed to a walk. The feeling of Roslyn in his arms was exquisite, and he wanted to prolong the experience as long as possible.

"Esther," she said, inexplicably, as they were passing Miss Lottie's cottage. He looked down at her questioningly, his heart thumping at how close her cheek was to his. "It's possible that Esther's engagement could be broken, and then you would be free to pursue her."

He would never understand how her mind worked. "What are you talking about?"

"Her fiancé is dangerous. I've seen the bruises on her arms, Miles. Once her parents understand how despicable he is, they won't want her falling into his care. Especially when they know that an equally wealthy viscount is interested in her."

"I'm not interested in her," he said, mildly outraged.

"You're not?"

"No!" he exploded, and tightened his arms around her for an instant for her foolishness.

"Oh." He saw a little smile play at her lips, the minx. "I thought you were."

"Well, I'm not. Nor am I wealthy, either."

"Oh, well, as to that. Of course you don't have vats of gold lying around, but you do have sufficient to keep Oakwood in excellent order." Mournfully, she added, "Unlike us."

"You don't know," he began, then set his jaw. Best to keep his mouth closed about his financial crisis. He'd kept the secret all these years; there was no reason to let it out now.

The remainder of the short journey passed in blessed silence. He stabled Damon while Roslyn went inside the house. Slowed by a conversation with the groom, he entered the hall at the same time Roslyn, who had donned a pretty green gown, was descending the stairs. She looked at him pensively, saying nothing; but after a fractional hesitation she accepted his arm, and he led her into the parlor.

"About time," commented Mr. Andrews, rising. "Luncheon was ready a quarter hour ago."

Jonathan came forward to greet Roslyn, and Miles relinquished his post without showing the reluctance he felt. Immediately Miss Sheridan sprang to take his arm, and the others stirred to follow them from the room.

"Oh, Miles," called Mr. Andrews in the hall. "Almost forgot. Your mother sent a footman with a message for you. Seems you have unexpected visitors. Mayhap you'd better read the note now in case it's urgent."

The viscount begged Colleen's pardon and walked to the hall table, where messages were kept on a silver tray. He could not imagine who would visit without warning. A glance at the note's spindly script gave hint of his mother's state of mind, and he frowned as he read. When he had finished, the note fell through his nerveless fingers to the floor.

"Is something wrong?" Roslyn asked, her eyes round with concern.

A distant part of him registered that while the others had gone into the dining room, she alone stood beside him.

"Yes," he whispered.

"No one has died!"

"Yes."

She took his arm. "Oh my dear!"

"No, no. That is, no one close . . . not a relative." His brow wrinkled. "Not precisely a relative, that is."

"Miles," she said, a hundred questions in her tone.

He studied her beloved face and wondered what the next moments would bring to their relationship. Perhaps now she wouldn't even want to be his friend. He had deceived her, after all, for years. Just as he had deceived his mother.

But now his mother knew something; the note hinted at it. After all his father had done, after all *he* had done, his mother would know the truth. And so would everyone, because of this death. And his unimaginable visitors.

He might as well tell Roslyn. He'd carried the truth in his heart like a dead, cold stone for years, and now he could carry it no longer.

"The man who died would have been my father-in-law in a few years," he said, his eyes fastened on Roslyn.

"Your father-in-law," she repeated, uncomprehending.

"Yes, when his daughter grew old enough to be married. She should be . . . oh, let me see. We were promised when I was twenty and Desiree twelve. So she would be sixteen now, I believe."

"You . . . were betrothed . . . to a twelve-year-old?"

"The wedding won't take place until she's passed her eighteenth birthday, so it's not as scandalous as you might think. The years aren't so far apart as yours and Jonathan's, you know."

"Don't speak to me of Jonathan," she said, her eyebrows lowering. "You're betrothed? And never told me?"

"You have it," he said, almost enjoying how much he hated himself. "And now my bride-to-be and her mother are waiting at Oakwood."

"Your fiancée is at Oakwood?"

She seemed to be having trouble comprehending what he was telling her, and he couldn't blame her. "Yes, it seems my betrothed has decided it's time to meet her future husband."

Roslyn stared at him, evidently too shocked to speak.

"So if you'll excuse me," he said, no longer able to meet her eyes, "I'll go home now and greet my future wife."

Eight

"I'm going with you," Roslyn stated, following Miles through the kitchen and out the back door. Her world had just been tossed on its head, and she was determined to find out why before another moment passed.

"No." His tone brooked no disagreement as he strode toward the stable. "This will be difficult enough without you."

Difficult? How could he speak of *his* difficulties when her mind was reeling like a whirlwind? All of her carefully laid plans to marry him off had been destroyed in the past few minutes.

But if he were to be married, an inner voice prompted as she raced along beside him, what did it matter to whom, so long as he was happy? That had been her intention in forming the house party from the start.

Yet it *did* matter, she told the voice, her jaw clenching. For years Miles had lied and lied and lied to her, making her think he held her in special regard. She would not trust him or her own judgment again.

When they reached the stable, he firmly moved

her aside and began saddling Damon. Roslyn struggled for words, finally saying, "Why, Miles? How could you do this?"

His face looking pale, he shook his head. "Nothing you would understand." He swung his leg over Damon and reined the horse from the stable. "Don't follow, Roslyn. Please."

Moved for an instant by his entreaty, she watched him ride away. But he owed her more than that. She called for Roger to harness the horse and gig.

By the time she entered the front hall of Oak-wood Castle, her courage had softened by several degrees. Jasper's pallid face did little to inspire her as he slowly led the way to the parlor, nor did the highly charged atmosphere in the room as she entered. She'd expected the look of outraged resignation in the viscount's eyes, but Lady Beaumont's discomposure shook her to the heart. Yet it was that good lady who performed introductions, albeit shakily.

The two strangers sitting opposite the viscount and his mother were both dressed in black. Roslyn briefly registered a thin, middle-aged woman before moving her attention to the younger one, whose fair complexion and flaxen hair were set to advantage against the dark finery of her gown. Desiree Highton was her name, Roslyn learned.

"How do you do," Miss Highton said, echoing her mother's extremely cultured tones, the accent unmistakably American. Her elegant features were dominated by a pair of large, blue eyes fringed with pale lashes. She was quite attractive,

Roslyn realized with a pang, although her face had an untried look, rather like an empty slate. But that, of course, was because she was so *young*. Not that she appeared girlish in any way. Her figure was well formed, and although the stranger was sitting, Roslyn gained the impression that she was taller than average height.

An uncomfortable pause alerted Roslyn that something was expected of her. "I—that is, Miles—I mean, Lord Beaumont mentioned briefly about Mr. Highton's passing. Please allow me to offer my condolences."

As both ladies bowed their heads, Lady Beaumont said, "How kind of you to offer your sympathy to our visitors."

"And so quickly, too," Miles said with a grim look. "I believe you were about to sit down to luncheon at Misthaven. Don't let us detain you."

"Why, Miles," exclaimed his mother. "Of course Roslyn must visit awhile. Please be seated, dear."

As Roslyn claimed the chair nearest Lady Beaumont, she felt an awkward silence falling over the group. She should leave. She really had no right to be there.

Yes, she did. Loving Miles gave her that right.

Loving Miles? She must have been mad to think it! He was untrustworthy. Nothing he'd ever said to her, nothing he'd ever implied, had meant a thing.

She stood abruptly. "I beg your pardon, but I must away. I know you have much to discuss."

The tears gathering in her eyes made her furious. "Good—good day."

Roslyn was turning to leave when Lady Beaumont seized her hand. "No, stay. You will know all eventually." Addressing the visitors, she added, "Roslyn is our neigbbor, and though she'll be leaving us soon—she's engaged to be married— she is like family to us. Speak as freely in her presence as you would in ours. I know we may depend upon her discretion."

Slowly, Roslyn sank into the chair, although not before Miles turned his back to the room to prod the fire with a poker. She felt his anger as surely as she did the heat of the flames.

Lady Beaumont continued. "Roslyn, you may be surprised to learn that Miss Highton—*Desiree*— has been engaged to wed my son for some time now." With unusual vigor she added, "I know *I* was surprised."

"My late husband was quite firm that we remain quiet about the betrothal for reasons I didn't understand until recently," explained Mrs. Highton. "As you can imagine, the situation caused my daughter and myself some distress. Neither of us had met Lord Beaumont."

Roslyn's incredulous gaze sought the viscount, who remained stubbornly occupied with the fireplace. "This is the first time you've met?" She asked.

Turning, Miles said in clipped tones, "My father and Mr. Highton arranged the marriage."

"But *why?*" Roslyn moaned. *And why did you consent to it?* she wanted to add.

"That's what I wondered as well," Desiree said.

Mrs. Highton glanced at her daughter. "Well, of course you knew your father always wanted a title in the family for the social validation." She dabbed at her eyes with her handkerchief and faced Lady Beaumont. "Arthur built his fortune in shipping, but he never forgot his roots. His people were very poor and ill educated. Because my family had greater advantages than his, he always felt the need to prove himself. That's why we came to England to live, to gain a superior education for our daughter and a more comfortable way of life in Society."

"But why did he forbid you to speak of the engagement?" Roslyn asked. "Was it because of Miss Highton's age?" *It should be,* she thought. All three of those gentlemen should be ashamed of themselves (and Miles, especially), arranging a child's life in such a way, giving her no choice in the matter as to how her future would proceed. This was not the Dark Ages.

"That is the question I've been wondering," commented Lady Beaumont.

"Arranged marriages aren't unusual, Mother," said Miles.

"But secret arrangements *are,*" Roslyn told him.

Mrs. Highton's gaze moved from Roslyn to Lady Beaumont, and finally to the viscount, whose cheeks flushed as he resumed stirring the logs.

"My husband told me long ago that it was not his desire to keep the matter secret," she said. "It

was Lord Beaumont's—your late husband's, I
mean."

Lady Beaumont looked perplexed. "My husband wished it to remain secret? But why?"

"Mr. Highton would not tell me no matter how
much I asked," said Mrs. Highton. "I didn't understand until two weeks ago, at the reading of
his will."

Miles replaced the poker into its stand with a
clatter. "Don't you think it best to honor your
husband's wishes?"

His mother stared at him, a harder look in her
eyes than Roslyn had believed the lady was capable of. "Miles, it's enough that your father kept
this from me. Will you compound his error and
yours by keeping me ignorant?"

And me as well, Roslyn wanted to add, but
thought it best to keep quiet at this point.

"My daughter and I didn't travel here to cause
dissention in your household," Mrs. Highton told
Lady Beaumont. "We were only concerned about
the future alliance between our families."

"Of course you were," said Lady Beaumont. "I
would feel the same."

"I didn't realize your husband had kept the arrangement secret from *you.* Once the will was read
and I understood matters, I assumed Lord Beaumont wanted to keep the knowledge from his *acquaintances.* When Desiree grew old enough to be
married, you see, she and your son were to carry
on what would appear to be a normal courtship.
The unpleasant details need never be known."

Roslyn's pulse accelerated as Lady Beaumont

said in a very quiet voice, "What unpleasant details?" She looked from Desiree to Mrs. Highton. When they appeared to shrink from her, she turned to her son. "Miles?"

Capitulating, he sat beside his mother and clasped her hands. The look of devastation in his eyes constricted Roslyn's breath.

"Father wanted to protect you," he said. "Do you remember how much he once enjoyed making wagers? And then he stopped?"

"Yes, of course. I thought he'd finally listened to my advice." She frowned. "Did he lose a great deal of money, Miles? Is that why he—" She glanced at Desiree, then back to her son. "He wanted you to marry well to maintain the estate?"

"Something like that," Miles said uneasily. He looked at Roslyn then, and she suddenly understood that he hadn't wanted this marriage, that he had sacrificed himself as she was sacrificing *herself*, both of them little more than currency in the ageless struggle to maintain property.

Not that marrying Jonathan was a sacrifice. He was eminently lovable. And Desiree appeared to be a prize any gentleman would be pleased to accept.

Matters were quite felicitious, in fact. Both she and Miles should be very happy with their separate futures.

If so, then why was she fighting tears?

"It is a little more complicated than that, I'm afraid," Mrs. Highton was saying. She appeared uncomfortable yet determined. "My late husband has been financing Oakwood Castle for the past four years, since the arrangement was made.''

''Since the betrothal,'' Lady Beaumont said numbly.

''Arthur redeemed the viscount's estate from debt,'' said the visitor, her voice lowering with sympathy. ''Your husband persuaded him to allow your family to continue as always, maintaining the pretense of owning Oakwood Castle. Arthur was not insistent upon taking control immediately, not so long as he knew we'd eventually be part of an aristocratic lineage through our daughter's marriage.''

''Taking control—'' Lady Beaumont's eyes sought her son's. ''Am I hearing correctly? We no longer own Oakwood?''

''No, milady,'' said Desiree in a clear, sweet voice that pierced Roslyn for its lack of emotion. ''Oakwood Castle belongs to me.''

Events blurred for Roslyn after that moment. She was distantly aware of people speaking, of the unusual sight of Lady Beaumont weeping, and the soothing murmur of the viscount's voice as he comforted his mother. Unable to bear the scene a second longer, she begged their pardon and hastened from the room. Jasper was not quick enough for her at the front door; thus she tried to open it herself. The simple action of turning a doorknob appeared beyond her capabilities, however. She twisted it in one direction, then the opposite, with no effect, and finally slapped the door in frustration.

"I'll drive you home," the viscount said, opening the door for her.

She shook her head, her heart too full to risk even a few moments alone with him. "Your guests," she said, her throat thick with tears.

"They'll understand." His voice sounded impossibly calm to her ears, even kind, which made her tears flow even faster. The last thing she wanted was for him to see her so distraught, but she couldn't refuse the gentle pressure of his hand on her arm as he guided her to the gig.

"Why didn't you tell me, Miles?" she asked as they lurched into motion. He looked at her briefly, then back at the road. "Oh. Your father swore you to secrecy, didn't he?"

After a fractional hesitation, Miles said, "Above all things, he dreaded my mother and your sire finding out."

Roslyn dashed tears from her eyes. "I vaguely recall my father arguing with yours about his gambling years ago."

"Yes, and he wouldn't listen until all was lost."

"But how could this happen? Wasn't there an entailment?"

Miles shook his head. "Somehow my ancestors avoided it. It seemed unnecessary. Preservation of the estate was bred into us."

Until your father, Roslyn thought, knowing Miles couldn't say the words because of loyalty. "How sorry I am that this happened. I know how much Oakwood means to you and Lady Beaumont." It was not a thing he talked about often, but she had always recognized his pride in the home where generations of Beaumonts had dwelled.

Her own home had been built by her grandfather. A house less than fifty years old was no house at all, in her opinion. When the wind blew eerily through Misthaven's eaves, she thought only of poor carpentry, never ghosts. There was no magic or mystery in a young home, but every shadowed corner and cubbyhole at Oakwood hinted of intrigue and secrets.

This put her in mind of Jonathan's estate, which boasted the newest manor in Chawton, the Leffews having attained wealth only a generation ago due to wise investments in a South American sugar plantation. On bright days, the yellow bricks of Foxtree House blinded visitors like a sun. When she married Jonathan, she would force ivy up the walls and encourage her husband to add a wing for architectural interest so the house would no longer resemble a box.

The thought brought a fresh round of tears. "Oh, Miles. I'm sorry for what I said earlier about your engagement to a child. Now I understand why you had to agree to it."

"Who said I agreed to it?" he stated angrily, as if the words had sought release for a long time.

"Your father made the arrangements without your consent?" she asked, her heart pounding in outrage.

Miles didn't speak for a moment as he directed the horse onto the road. "He felt there was no other choice," he said finally, sounding calmer.

"When Highton offered the solution, he couldn't refuse his only chance to keep Oakwood in the family." The faint lines at the sides of his mouth deepened. "To do Father justice, he believed my affections were unattached."

Roslyn's breath caught in her throat as she calculated the timing of her companion's betrothal. Miles had begun to pay court to her—or so she had believed—four years ago. Then suddenly his interest had cooled. Now she understood why, or at least thought she did.

"And were your affections unattached?" she asked softly as he pulled the gig onto Misthaven's drive. She wished he would drive slower; within moments they would have to part.

"What would it matter if they were? I hadn't declared myself."

"You were only twenty, Miles. I suppose you thought there was time."

He did not respond to this as he drew the carriage to a halt in front of her home. After he assisted her down, she clung to his arm as they walked up the steps, then stayed his hand as he reached for the door. For once she hoped Marsden would be as slow to his duties as he often was.

"There's no hope that the two of you won't suit," she said, her mind rapidly searching for solutions.

"Miss Highton may find me not to her liking; it wouldn't surprise me in the least."

She waved her hand dismissively. "Unthinkable."

"You put me to the blush." Even at such a moment as this, he could make her smile. As he continued, however, her grin faltered. "But consider if she didn't want to marry me. Suppose she's met someone. You heard her; Oakwood is her property."

"She could . . ." Roslyn could not bring the words to her lips.

"Evict us," Miles finished.

Roslyn pressed her temples. "I can't believe this is happening."

"Had Arthur Highton lived, the secret could have been maintained. Now that Oakwood has fallen into the hands of a young girl, the future can't be guessed."

"She will have to wait until she attains her majority before making changes, surely."

He shrugged as if beyond caring. "One can hope."

"And you would never try to break the engagement yourself," she said, knowing the answer. "Even if your home wasn't at risk. You couldn't breach your father's promise."

"No more than you could break your promise to Jonathan," he said.

"Honor," she breathed, hating the word.

He nodded. "There are some things more important than one's own desires."

And what are *your desires?* she longed to ask him, but refrained, for nothing could be gained by such conversation but further hurt. How she admired his integrity. That he had kept his father's shameful secret all these years must have been unimaginably difficult. The hurt she had been carrying with her since she was seventeen and had thought him cynical, cold, unreliable in matters of the heart . . . all of that was gone. In some way she must have known he was a man of excellent character all along, for she had never stopped loving him. She could admit that now.

It was possible that he no longer felt toward her as he had. As he said, he'd never truly declared himself to her. Perhaps her feelings were unreciprocated. But she didn't believe she could be so mistaken. Fine though his character might be, Miles had no patience for people he didn't like. And he'd never been able to leave her alone, had he? Always visiting, always teasing and making her laugh. She could almost laugh at this moment for the joy of knowing he'd not deliberately abandoned her, if the loss of their future together didn't loom so painfully.

He must have read her thoughts in her eyes, for he backed away a step. "I apologize for not being able to continue providing escort to your guests, but my major occupation must now be entertaining my own."

"No, no." She couldn't bear the thought of being separated from him now. These last few weeks were all they had. "Bring Miss Highton here."

"Roslyn, aside from the awkwardness of our situation, she's in mourning. And don't forget her age. She's hardly old enough to leave the nursery."

"No one needs to know her age," she said in firm tones. "She looks much older than sixteen.

And who will object to a young lady seeking conversation in the country? I'm not planning another ball, so it's not as though she'd be expected to dance. I'll make sure our activities are very sedate."

"I don't think that's a wise plan, Roslyn."

"Well, I do. If she'll come, bring her. If she won't, then visit alone."

Before he could protest further, she kissed him quickly on the lips, then opened the door and rushed inside.

Nine

During the next few days, Miles occupied himself with showing the estate to Mrs. Highton and her daughter. Accompanied by his mother, the viscount and the Hightons visited every cottage and met with each tenant, explaining only that the Hightons were friends of the family, all parties agreeing to the wisdom of maintaining silence about their circumstances for the time being. When they had exhausted the boundaries of the property, he and his mother led the ladies through the castle, explaining the history of each room and stories behind many of the furnishings that had been collected through the decades.

He quite deliberately avoided Misthaven. Despite Roslyn's request, he had no plans to twist his heart into knots by being near her. However well intentioned, however innocent, her kiss had settled the issue. He could not forget the sweet pressure of her lips. In that instant when Roslyn kissed him, only the tightest control had prevented him from crushing her to him and smothering her with kisses of his own, which would not have been at all innocent. He would not subject himself to that torture again.

But on Thursday morning at breakfast, Jasper delivered a note to Lady Beaumont that filled the viscount with foreboding.

"The Andrews have invited us to tea this afternoon," she said, her gaze settling first on him, then Mrs. Highton. "I don't know if you feel ready for a social gathering, Jocelyn. I bow to your judgment in this. I'll go only if you wish to attend."

"I confess I'm too tired for it," said the lady. "Since Arthur has left us, I have no energy. But Desiree may wish to go. It's all right with me if you do, child."

"I think it should be very pleasant," said Desiree.

Miles uttered an oath beneath his breath. There was no possible way to avoid Misthaven now, nor to dampen the memory of Roslyn's kiss. He gritted his teeth at the prospect of watching her with Jonathan. Jonathan, a man no one could dislike, yet Miles kept fighting an image of himself strangling him.

One consolation kept him from utter despair; his future wife and her mother made pleasant companions. Despite the potential for ill feelings, Lady Beaumont and Mrs. Highton appeared to be forging a friendship. And Desiree's quiet, intelligent manner belied her young age. There was nothing embarrassingly girlish about her, no childish giggles or silly questions. She owned a serenity he envied.

There were disadvantages to her self-possession,

of course. When compared to Roslyn's vivacity and fire, Desiree's silences made him restless. He recalled Roslyn warning him once that he would become bored with such a woman. It was not boredom that troubled his time with Desiree so much as the fact that, after three days, he knew little more about her than he had in their first moments together.

She made a striking companion, though, there was no doubting that, he thought that afternoon at Misthaven as Marsden led the two of them to the south garden where tables and chairs had been placed for tea. Desiree's silk gown was black for mourning, but its capped sleeves were caught up with pink rosettes, as was the high collar. Morbid though it seemed, the colors could not have been more perfect to set off her understated blond beauty.

As soon as they appeared on the terrace, Roslyn jumped from her table to join them. Had he any doubts as to his assessment of Desiree's loveliness, Roslyn's instant, frowning appraisal would have reassured him. How sweetly she amused him with her transparent emotions. He had been able to read her moods since boyhood.

Roslyn led them from one table to the next, introducing her guests to Desiree, then at last commanding they join Jonathan, Esther, Gregory, and herself at a round table decorated with white linen and a bouquet of wildflowers. Miles complied with silent reservations. He knew Roslyn had planned this meeting down to the last detail, the little vixen, and he was helpless to do a thing about it.

Jonathan spoke first. "How long have you lived in England, Miss Highton?"

"For six years now," Desiree said. "I suppose my accent gave me away."

"No, no . . . though it's quite charming," Jonathan said. "Roslyn told me you came from America."

"I've lived in England long enough to feel as if I were born here, but I doubt I shall ever sound like it."

"And I suppose in all that time you've never had a family portrait made, or perhaps a miniature of your parents inside a locket," Roslyn said abruptly, her tone so accusing that she drew every eye at the table. Miles studied her warily, knowing something was behind the question, though he could not dream what.

If Desiree was surprised by the query, she covered it well. "My mother and I posed when I was very small, but Papa was always too busy."

"Naturally he was," Roslyn said, giving Miles a significant look, which he returned with raised brows. Whatever she was thinking, he felt certain he didn't want to know.

Jonathan gave a bewildered smile. "Why all this . . . interest in a portrait?"

"I just find it odd that there has never been a time when Miles met with all the Hightons *together*."

"That doesn't seem odd to me," Esther said. "I've known you for years and years, yet not until this week have I met your father nor seen a portrait of the two of you."

"Yes, but you—" Roslyn looked down in confusion, seeming to catch herself. Moments later she glanced up with a look of relief. "Good, here's Marsden with tea. Cook made her specialty this afternoon, scones with strawberry glaze. You'll . . . like . . ."

Roslyn was staring at something in the distance. Miles looked and saw Harriet Pollehn running toward them, her poke bonnet lifting in the breeze like a sail. Roger Crim followed at her heels, but stopped suddenly as he saw the tea tables and well-dressed company.

"Oh, gorsh," the groom said, and reversed direction.

"Has anyone seen Three?" Harriet cried.

Seated with Colleen, Victoria, and Ned, Thurmond Andrews shouted, "Have you lost those accursed cats again?"

"Only Three!"

"That's three too many!" he cried. Miles couldn't prevent a grunt of laughter, though he sympathized with Thurmond's ire.

"I'm sorry, Mr. Andrews," Harriet called, her head moving back and forth as she scanned the bushes and wildflowers, "but I only wanted to look in on them before coming to tea. They get so lonely in the stable! I have no idea how Three got loose!"

"Oh, good heavens," Roslyn said in irritation.

"Perhaps our mysterious jewel thief set them—him—free," called Colleen with a laugh.

"Jewel thief?" Desiree asked, turning to Miles with an inscrutable look. He wondered if she was thinking what he often did, that Misthaven resembled a madhouse.

A sudden, rolling growl brought all conversation to a halt. So threatening was the sound, so wild, that Miles felt instantly alert, as if he'd been transported to the African veldt in the blink of an eye and now must protect them all. Before he could move, however, Esther slid from her chair and glided in the direction of the noise.

He was on his feet in a heartbeat, as was Jonathan. Leffew surprised him at the rapidity of his speech when he said, "No, Miss Cummings. That animal sounds dangerous."

"Cats don't frighten me," she said, smiling, and pointed to a bulge in the wildflowers moving stealthily toward the east. Ignoring their protests, she walked quietly toward the furtive animal. Miles began to circle to her left, hoping to halt the beast if it bolted.

"Oh, please catch him, catch him," Harriet begged. "But don't hurt him."

"I'm trying, Harriet," Esther said.

The cat was now visible to Miles. He saw it stop dead and glare at Miss Cummings.

"Back away, Esther," Miles whispered. He had never sensed such anger from an animal. But there was no dissuading her. Looking inexpressibly sweet, she bent toward the cat and murmured coaxing words. At once, the animal howled and lashed the young lady's arms with extended claws, then ran.

"Oh . . . my," Esther said faintly, the color draining from her face.

Miles moved forward, but the cat was closer to Jonathan. "Beast!" cried that gentleman, diving for the animal and managing to catch its hind legs. The cat coiled backward like a spring, launching front claws and teeth at Leffew's head and shoulders until he was forced to let go.

With freedom came complete madness. Instead of running for the wood and possible escape, the cat sprang into the midst of the gentlemen and ladies. After darting among boots and slippers, he jumped atop a table and scattered cups and saucers, then leaped down to skitter away from the grasp of the gentlemen who bounded after him with red faces and yells of frustration.

Joining the fray, Miles had time to note that while Harriet screamed, Colleen howled with laughter, and Victoria grasped Mr. Andrews's arm as if terrified. And then Roslyn delighted him by grabbing the vase off her table and aiming it carefully. The shot fell short of its goal; nevertheless, the black-and-white cat streaked across the terrace, into the flowers, and disappeared.

"Good try!" he said.

Instead of looking gratified, she was coming toward him with a very intent expression. He had time to see Desiree leave the table with Gregory, the two of them slowly following the beast's trail, before Roslyn arrived, a sheen of perspiration making her skin glow beautifully.

"Come with me a moment," she whispered in

urgent tones, taking his arm. "I must speak with you. Pretend we're looking for the cat."

"Hadn't you better take care of Esther?" he said.

She tossed an impatient look toward her friend. "Jonathan is looking out for her."

He certainly was, Miles noted with surprise. Esther's outstretched arms were cradled in Leffew's hands as he examined her scratches while she, standing on tiptoes, looked with horror at the streaks of blood on his forehead. The viscount frowned at the tender scene and wondered that Roslyn hadn't noted it.

This was an aspect of Leffew that he'd never considered, that the *very proper gentleman* might be light with his affections— perhaps even a womanizer. If so, he'd best change. Miles wouldn't permit Roslyn to be hurt.

"I've wanted to speak with you this age," Roslyn said, pulling him onto the graveled path that wound among the stands of flowers. "Are you avoiding us? It's been days and days since I last saw you."

"You know the reason as well as I do, Roslyn."

She scowled, looking so adorable he wanted to kiss the frown lines away. "Yes, and your visitors are the very reason I need to speak with you." She stopped and faced him, clutching both of his arms for an instant as if to seize every inch of his attention. No worry there; he couldn't look away. Lowering her voice to a whisper, she continued. "Have you considered that Mrs. Highton and her daughter might be imposters?"

He had, in fact, considered it. That Roslyn should think of it as well was no surprise. He doubted her mind and imagination ever paused for breath.

"They're not imposters," he said.

"How can you be sure? I believe you said you'd never met either of the ladies. What if Mr. Highton is still alive? Your visitors could have found out about the proposed marriage of convenience through a servant in the household. Or perhaps the real Desiree told her friends about it, and one of them hatched this scheme with her mother. If the lady who claims to be Mrs. Highton is her mother, that is. There are a hundred ways they could—"

"Roslyn, would you please stop a moment?" he asked, grinning, and closed his hands over hers. "Listen to me. There's nothing to be gained. The estate belongs to the Hightons, if you recall. Why should an imposter want to wed a penniless viscount with no place to call home?"

She didn't speak for a few seconds, though he sensed thoughts moving behind her eyes. "Perhaps they sought a title for some reason. Maybe Desiree has a strong need to be married; perhaps she's escaping a horrible situation at home—"

"Roslyn—"

"*Or* perhaps you're not penniless after all," she added with gathering excitement. "What if a relative has left you a bequest, and you don't know about it yet!"

"And Desiree does," he said, shaking his head.

"Why would she know about my bequest before I do?"

"Well, I don't know, Miles! I can't think of everything!"

He stared at her, his smile remaining idiotically in place. How in thunder was he going to live without this maddening woman? She had the power to bring his blood to the boiling point, even in the midst of her most illogical arguments. He almost gathered her in his arms then, but his awareness of the people surrounding them stayed the impulse. Instead, he settled for pressing his fingertips to her lips.

"If it will make you feel more at ease," he said gently, "I'll write our solicitor. He knows them and will be able to verify or disprove their claim."

"Good." Her gaze lowered to his hand, and he hastily withdrew it. "That's all I was asking you to do, to be cautious."

"I'm trying, Roslyn," he breathed, his gaze locking with hers. "I'm trying to be cautious, but it's not easy."

The desperate hope that leapt to her eyes told him she understood his message. He felt shame that he'd allowed himself that moment of weakness. It could accomplish nothing.

When Desiree suddenly appeared beside him with Gregory, Miles stepped back guiltily. Fortunately, the girl did not appear to notice anything amiss.

"The cat may be lost," she said.

Miles managed to look grave. "What appalling news."

Gregory grinned at him. "Last we saw it, the mad thing was running for the woods."

Desiree gave the gentlemen a measuring look, and Miles felt momentarily reproved. "Miss Pollehn has gone to look for him," she said. "Everyone else is giving up. She seems very distressed."

Roslyn sighed. "I'd better find her." Giving Miles a regretful glance, she moved away. She had not gone two steps before she swerved around. "Since our tea has been ruined, I insist you stay for dinner."

"No, that's not—" Miles began.

"How delightful," Desiree said at the same moment. She looked at him, hesitating.

"Whatever you like," he said reluctantly.

"Then I should be pleased to stay if we can send Mama a note. I am enjoying myself so much!"

By the following Saturday evening, Miles understood the terrible truth. Serene though she might be, Desiree took what seemed to him a perverse pleasure in the personalities gathered at Misthaven. He could see how it would be for the next week. He was going to be forced to attend the house party to its bitter end. They had not missed an event since Thursday, thanks to Roslyn's incessant invitations and Desiree's determined acceptances.

As he glanced at the faces gathered around Misthaven's dining table that night at dinner, he wondered what the coming years would bring for Roslyn and himself. How difficult it was to avoid returning his glance to her again and again. Of course she was not helping by outshining every lady in the room. She looked beyond enchanting in a lavender gown that followed the lines of her body like the hands of a lover. Every time their eyes met, he found it more wrenching to glance away. This house party was a deuced plague, forcing them to be near one another so much. Although their paths would doubtless cross many times in the future, at least it would not be so frequently.

Not for the first time he wondered why she'd wanted this strange assortment of people around her during her final weeks as an unmarried woman. Most young ladies would be planning their weddings down to the last detail instead of coordinating activities for one of the most disparate groups of human beings he'd ever met.

He had to admit that Roslyn's grace in doing so surprised him. If ever he'd thought her the slightest bit self-absorbed, her behavior during the past week had removed that misconception. One had only to observe her patience in dealing with that odd Miss Pollehn to see. In the manner of the most accomplished hostess, Roslyn was at this very moment trying to draw her into the conversation, a daunting effort given the spinster's thundercloud demeanor.

"You've hardly eaten a thing, Harriet," Roslyn was saying. "Is the lamb not to your liking? I'll have Cook bring whatever you like."

Harriet shook her head as she ran her fork across her vegetables. "I'll never see Three again."

"Pray God that it's so," said Mr. Andrews.

Roslyn's eyes met the viscount's with an immediate spark of humor, but her tone was chiding as she said, "Oh, Father, you don't mean that."

"Strike me if I don't." He served himself another helping of lamb from the platter that Marsden held before him. "Don't mean to hurt the girl, but that cat's earned its freedom. Probably a hundred times happier now than he was cooped up in that cage."

"You don't understand," Harriet said. "My work on social isolation was destroyed when he escaped. I would have freed him after the experiment. My entire purpose was to observe how he behaved after being separated from his friends for several weeks and then reunited."

Mr. Andrews grunted. "Seems to me you saw that. Drove him mad as a bat."

Miles, noting Miss Pollehn's face darken, said quickly, "How are your scratches healing, Esther?"

"You can hardly see them," she said. "I know the cat only lashed out because he was frightened. He could have hurt me much worse if he wished."

Jonathan touched his forehead tentatively. "My scars are fading, too, I believe."

"I'm so glad," Esther said, her gaze consuming his face. Jonathan's eyes linked with hers. He smiled.

Miles shot a swift look at Roslyn, who was talking to Colleen and oblivious of this interchange. "How fortunate," he said loudly. "The marks should be entirely gone by your wedding, Jonathan. Hard to believe it's only a few weeks away. The second Saturday in June, isn't it?"

He felt like a brute when Roslyn shot him a puzzled, hurt look, but the comment seemed necessary to remind Jonathan of where his loyalties lay. Miles was gratified when Leffew shifted his attention to Roslyn and began to speak of the wedding trellis arch he'd ordered to be made. It was to be painted white and laced with roses, and he and Roslyn would stand under it to recite their vows in chapel. Utter rot that, Miles thought. He should have left well enough alone.

He closed his ears and returned to his roasted lamb and potatoes, but soon he felt the uncomfortable sensation that Desiree was watching him. He often sensed her eyes upon him, both here and at Oakwood. A natural thing to do, he imagined, for a young girl who was contemplating her future. Fortunately, she didn't appear displeased with him.

On the other hand, she seemed equally satisfied when in the company of anyone else. Thus he felt uneasy when falling under her scrutiny. He imagined her weighing him against some lad she knew in London and finding him wanting.

"Please convey my compliments to the cook," Victoria Pendergrass said to Marsden in such regal tones that the viscount's attention was captured. Turning to Mr. Andrews, who sat on her left at the table's head, she added, "I have never tasted more tender lamb. How is it you've assembled such exemplary servants from this small village, sir? They could grace London's finest town house."

Roslyn instantly came to attention. "Have you ever lived in a London town house, Victoria?"

Miss Pendergrass returned her look with perfect composure. "Why, no, I haven't, Roslyn, but I've visited friends who do; and let me assure you, they would be pleased with a household that runs itself so efficiently."

"Well," said Andrews, evidently confused but gratified nevertheless. "Well, now. Must say my late wife did the hiring. Can't take credit when it's not mine."

"But she asked for your approval before employing them, did she not? I cannot believe she wouldn't seek your advice."

The viscount's mouth twisted with irony as Andrews's eyes grew vague. "Now that you mention it," said the older gentleman, "I do believe she did. Is that not right, Marsden? Did I approve the hirings?"

For the first time in his memory, Miles saw the butler appear unsure of himself. He covered with a cough and answered, "I can't recall, sir."

Roslyn's father speared a chunk of meat into his mouth and gave his companion a friendly look as he chewed. "Good of you to mention it, Vicky."

Eyes narrowing, Roslyn turned a pointed look at the viscount as if to say, *You see how it is?* He lifted his shoulders ever so slightly and raised his brows: *I do, but what is there to be done?*

And then he felt Desiree's eyes upon him again. He forced a smile and returned to his plate. She looked so thoughtful. What was she thinking behind those placid blue eyes?

Had Desiree's father lived, he would have forced her to carry through with the betrothal. Now she had no reason to do so. She already owned Oakwood, and she didn't seem particularly desirous of being called viscountess. He hoped loyalty to her sire's memory would keep her faithful to his promise. If not, he and his mother would have to leave.

He almost wished Roslyn's suspicions would prove true, that Desiree and her mother were imposters. It would only delay the inevitable; he still would have to wed someone he didn't love. But at least his mother could live out her days in the home she loved.

In response to Roslyn's plea, he had penned a letter to the family solicitor and sent it off yesterday. But he held little hope that he'd find Desiree was anyone but who she claimed to be.

A sudden pounding interrupted his worries. Marsden, occupied with arranging dishes on the sideboard, wiped his hands on a cloth and eased from the room.

The loud knocking sounded so urgent that conversations around the table ceased. Hearing Marsden open the front door and speak to someone, Miles tilted his head. A masculine voice, raspy and demanding, responded. The butler's tone rose. The stranger replied, sounding nearer. Feeling danger approaching, Miles rose to his feet, as did the other gentlemen.

A young man strode into the dining room, his jacket and pantaloons travel-stained, his thatch of blond hair disheveled. Marsden marched along beside him, apologizing to Mr. Andrews and the company for the intrusion, saying that the stranger had not listened to him.

Ignoring the butler, Mr. Andrews said in threatening tones, "Who are you, sir, and what do you want?"

The man's wild eyes scanned the table, then settled upon one young lady.

"Esther!" he cried.

"Braxton," she breathed, her face blanching.

Miss Cummings's fiancé. Miles felt an instant surge of anger. He'd been too preoccupied with his own concerns of late to think overmuch about the young lady's story and her fears that her betrothed would be looking for her; but now it all came back. He recalled his pledge to speak with this ruffian, and determined to remove him from the room at once. But Jonathan was faster than he.

"We've been expecting you, Mr. Ames," Leffew said, a chilly smile at his lips.

"Have you?" returned the stranger. Until this instant he had not removed his gaze from Esther, but now his eyes tore from hers to scan the hostile faces regarding him around the table. Taking in the aggressive postures of the gentlemen, he underwent a swift transformation, threading his fingers through his hair, straightening his jacket, and even attempting a halfhearted smile. "I apologize for my unconventional entry, but I've been searching for Esther for days." He gave Miss Cummings an admonishing look. "I've been half out of my mind, and your parents are beside themselves with worry."

"But I wrote them," she said faintly.

"Yes, you said you were going to a friend in Chawton," he chided, "but you didn't name the friend."

Her gaze fell to her plate. "I thought they would remember."

"Well, they didn't. I've been to every inn and large house within a twenty-mile radius."

"I'm sorry, Braxton."

"There's no reason for you to be sorry," Roslyn said, bravely staring down the stranger. A flare of admiration swept through the viscount. He relished seeing Roslyn's fiery spirit put to use in defense of her friend.

Braxton paid her no heed, his eyes flickering from Miles to Jonathan. "Come, Esther; we can discuss it on the journey back. Time to go home."

The silence became even more fraught with tension. Esther braced her hands on the table, started to rise, then sank into the chair, as if her legs had turned to water beneath her.

"No," she whispered.

"No?" He sounded as if he couldn't believe his ears.

"No, Braxton." This time she sounded more forceful. She lifted her eyes to his, and Miles had an inkling of what it must be costing her to keep her gaze steady. "I don't want to go with you."

The stranger's eyes flashed, all pretensions at civility dropping away. Miles sensed how deeply his anger ran when Ames said, "But you must. You're promised to me, and your family expects you."

"She doesn't have to leave if she doesn't wish!" Roslyn declared.

"No, indeed," chimed her father. "You're not wed yet. Only her parents have the right to remove her from beneath my roof."

The stranger's face flushed. "But I express the wishes of her sire."

Jonathan began to circle the table. "Miss Cummings has spoken her mind. She doesn't want to go with you."

Miles had never heard gentle Jonathan sound so sinister, and he couldn't forestall a look of surprise at his neighbor. Never in his life would he have imagined Leffew's eyes could appear so resolute or hostile.

Ames bristled. "She has no choice."

"I beg to differ," Miles said, standing beside Jonathan.

Ames turned disdainful eyes toward his betrothed. "I see you've worked your charms to advantage, Esther. What have you promised these men for such eager loyalty?"

Cries of outrage sounded around the table. Miles and Jonathan, both muttering angrily although the viscount would never recall what either of them said, each seized an arm and lifted the struggling man toward the door.

"Wait!" Esther cried, rising. "Please don't make him angry." She swept toward the men, one hand raised toward Jonathan begging restraint, her gaze centered on Ames. "Hear me, Braxton, please. Roslyn is my dearest friend, and I wanted only to visit her one last time before you and I wed. I ran away because I knew Papa and you wouldn't permit me to go. Her party lasts only one more week, and then I shall come home on my own, I promise." When he started to object, she said quickly, "Or if you wish, you can accompany me home at that time, and I will go willingly. Please, Braxton. Allow me to visit my friends from Montrose. I haven't seen them in years."

Miles felt rage pouring through Ames's body as the man's glaring eyes switched from Esther to Jonathan and himself. Finally, he freed his arms and straightened his shoulders.

"One week," he said. "I'll bring a carriage Saturday morning."

Miles felt his heart dip at the relief that swept over Esther's expression. "Thank you, Braxton," she said humbly.

Leaving nothing to chance, the viscount and Jonathan escorted Ames to the front door, and did not speak until they saw him riding away into the night. Returning inside, Leffew threw Miles a smoldering look.

"Does such an animal call himself a gentleman, I wonder?" he asked, his face grim.

"We'll speak with him when he comes next

week. I trust he'll be calmer then. Perhaps if he knows Esther has the protection of her friends, he'll treat her more kindly."

"Perhaps," said Jonathan, but the viscount felt he wasn't aware of what he said. He looked very far away.

Ten

"What is love?"

Roslyn's gaze flew to the vicar. It was Sunday morning; she was sitting in chapel, and until this moment she'd participated in worship without awareness, a not uncommon occurrence. Today, however, she had an excuse for her dreaming; her mind was occupied by a stormy wasteland of concerns. In addition to her personal dilemma, she feared desperately for Esther's future, which seemed a darker and more serious version of her own.

But now the vicar's question pierced her, and she grew alert.

The vicar continued: "We read in I Corinthians, Chapter Thirteen, about this subject: *"Though I bestow all my goods to feed the poor . . . and have not love, it profiteth me nothing."*

Roslyn cut a glance at Miles, who was sitting across the aisle with Desiree, his mother, and Mrs. Highton. She recalled her feeble attempts to win the servants' favor over the past weeks. Love had motivated her actions well enough, but not love for the servants. She'd wanted only to impress the viscount, to make herself admirable in his eyes. The servants must have sensed the insincerity of her emotions. It was little wonder they had responded so poorly to her.

Love never faileth, continued the vicar, looking earnestly at his congregation. The portly gentleman's mouth continued to move, but Roslyn heard no more.

She would never fail to love Miles, she knew that. She would be a good wife to Jonathan, but he would never lay claim to her heart. She lifted sad eyes to her betrothed, who sat at her left with Esther on his other side. Feeling her gaze, Jonathan winked and pressed her hand. Roslyn responded with a weak smile. She was being terribly unfair to this kind man. From this moment on, she must give him her undivided devotion.

But when chapel ended and the congregants filed outside the stone building, she couldn't slow her pounding heart as Miles approached with Desiree on his arm. He seemed more concerned with Esther than herself, however.

"You're looking well," he said to her.

"It's kind of you to say so, but I'm afraid I look tired," Esther responded. "It was difficult to sleep last night."

"I imagined as much, and I'm sorry for it," the viscount sympathized.

"Your betrothed is a dangerous man," Jonathan told Esther bluntly, looking very forbidding. "Perhaps you should speak to your parents. Or I would be happy to do so, as I'm sure Beaumont would."

"It would do no good," Esther said. "Roslyn and I were up most of the night talking but found no answers."

She was making a valiant effort to look optimistic, Roslyn thought, her throat constricting. A light sprinkle of freckles across Esther's upturned nose made her appear more fetching, not less, beneath her pink bonnet. *No wonder the gentlemen are so protective of her. She is as innocent as a child.*

"Up so late, both of you?" The viscount's eyes shifted to Roslyn, making her pulse leap like a rabbit at the warm expression she saw there. "And no circles under your eyes, either."

"Will you and Desiree join us this afternoon?" she asked quickly, anxious to change the subject. "I thought after luncheon we might all take a ride."

"I'd like that," Desiree said, "but will we return in time for evening chapel? I don't want to miss the service. Vicar Wainwright is an effective minister."

Miles appeared as surprised as Roslyn felt. Attending services twice in one day seemed excessively virtuous. "We can manage to be back in time," he said, the reluctance in his voice making her want to laugh. "We'll be over after luncheon, Roslyn."

At that moment, Harriet appeared at Roslyn's side and tugged her arm. "A moment alone with you, please!" she whispered urgently.

Forestalling a sigh, Roslyn excused herself and stepped apart with Harriet. "Brace yourself," said her guest, her small eyes boring into Roslyn's. "Colleen is wearing my butterfly brooch."

"What?"

"You know of what I'm speaking. The thefts? We've all been missing jewelry, and now I think I know the culprit."

Roslyn turned horrified eyes upon Colleen, who was standing some distance away listening to Ned's every word with eager nods and smiles. Upon the lacework bodice of her gown lay a pin in the shape of a butterfly, its stones glimmering in brilliant colors beneath the sunlight.

Roslyn didn't want to believe it. Couldn't. It was true her friend seemed even less inhibited than she had at the Academy, and sometimes her earthy humor embarrassed Roslyn, but it was a serious jump from that to thievery.

"I thought you said you were missing a *cat* brooch."

"Cats are not the only things in my life. I like butterflies, too."

"I—I don't know what to say."

"I understand you're shocked, but I want to know what you're going to *do* about it. She can't be allowed to take my things and wear them so brazenly."

"I'll talk to her later in private. Perhaps there's a logical explanation."

"Oh, I think there's a logical explanation all right. Colleen is a thief."

Luncheon passed uncomfortably for Roslyn, who could not prevent her eyes from returning repeatedly to the butterfly clinging to Colleen's dress like a brand of dishonor. The pin did not seem especially valuable, as the stones appeared to be made of glass. What could have possessed Colleen to do such a thing?

Harriet did nothing to make the meal easier. She shifted her eyes back and forth from Colleen to Roslyn, vexing her greatly. Did she expect her hostess to confront a guest in front of everyone?

Finally, Colleen herself precipitated matters. "Why is everyone staring at my"—an embarrassed giggle as she glanced at the gentlemen—"my neck?"

"I was looking at your brooch," Harriet said.

Colleen appeared pleased, slanting her eyes from one gentleman to the next as if the compliment had come from them. "Oh, do you like my butterfly? I call him Romeo."

"Romeo," Harriet repeated, sounding disgusted. "Where did you get him—I mean, *it?*"

"Harriet, please," Roslyn entreated. "We can talk about this later."

Colleen's head tilted curiously. "I don't mind telling her, Roslyn. One of my friends at home gave it to me."

Miss Pollehn pointed her finger accusingly. "You lie. That pin is *mine.*"

Colleen's mouth opened in shock. "It most certainly is *not!* I've had this brooch for years!"

"Here, what's this?" Mr. Andrews said, at the same moment signaling Marsden to bring him a second helping of plum pudding.

Victoria smiled and leaned toward the older gentleman, displaying her bosom to his fascinated notice as she often did, Roslyn saw, her ire doubling. "Don't be disturbed, Mr. Andrews. All young ladies squabble from time to time. Pay them no mind; they'll work it out."

"How matronly you've become since we graduated from Montrose," said Roslyn, hearing how snide she sounded but unable to stop herself.

"My dear," said Jonathan, his voice inflecting with gentle reproof.

Roslyn felt flames shooting through her head. Did he dare to correct her before it was his legal right? She would give him the only response he deserved; she would ignore him.

Returning her gaze to Victoria, she said, "It's true. Your actions and words are much older than someone of our years, I think. Don't you agree, Father? Don't you sometimes forget that Victoria is the same age as your daughter?"

Mr. Andrews, his startled eyes locking with Roslyn's, strained to swallow a mouthful of pudding. "How's that? What?"

Victoria straightened. "I've always felt older than my years, but perhaps that comes from being the eldest in a family with five children. I spent much of my youth looking after them."

The wounded look she shot down the table gave Roslyn a twinge of guilt, but she wouldn't recant. Not when her contemporary—her *friend*— had so obviously set her cap for Roslyn's father. There was no longer any use trying to explain it away as a guest trying to be polite to an elder host; Victoria seldom so much as deigned to speak to the younger gentlemen. Roslyn could almost think it a good thing the viscount's father had found a bride for his son on his own, because Miss Pendergrass showed Miles little interest at all.

Even if Miles hadn't already been engaged to Desiree, Roslyn was beginning to believe her house party had been doomed from the start. None of the young ladies had captured an edge of his attention, with the exception of Esther. And Esther herself was betrothed.

Victoria must be mad, preferring an ancient gentleman (no matter how dear to Roslyn, but that was because he was her father) over the handsome viscount.

In the years following her mother's death, Roslyn had often observed widows and spinsters trying to catch her father's attention to no avail, for he remained true to the memory of his beloved wife. Still, had he decided to fight loneliness by wedding one of those older ladies, Roslyn would have understood. But this flirtation of Victoria's was beyond understanding.

"What does it matter how old she acts?" Harriet declared. "The important thing is that I want my pin back."

Colleen threw her napkin on the table. "Are you accusing me of stealing? I cannot believe it!"

"No one has stolen anything, surely," Esther said. "Oh, I know what it must be. You both own similar pins!"

Harriet frowned. "Then why does she have *hers* and I don't have *mine*? You know *someone* in this house has been stealing jewelry, Esther, and I'll warrant a search of Colleen's things will reveal all!"

"You wish to search my room?" Colleen leaned back and gestured expansively. "Then do so. We'll settle this straightaway."

"Here now," said Mr. Andrews. "No need for that. Won't hear of people accusing my guests. No, indeed."

Colleen stood. "I don't mind, sir, truly I don't. I won't be comfortable if there's the slightest suspicion about my character."

"No one is suspicious—" Roslyn began.

"Good," said Harriet, rising. "I'll go. Who goes with me?"

There was an uneasy shrinking into chairs as Harriet's baleful eyes scanned the table.

Colleen's chin rose. "I'd prefer if all the ladies join us. Someone needs to verify my honesty besides Harriet, who has apparently lost her senses."

After this remark, there was nothing to be done except follow. Esther rose reluctantly, Victoria appeared to have lost patience as she crumpled her napkin and threw it beside her plate, and Roslyn trailed behind, wondering how her friends could have changed so much.

Or had they? Maybe she was the one who'd become different. Perhaps her judgment had altered over these few years. Only Esther seemed nearly the same.

It was an awkward assemblage in Colleen's room. Roslyn had selected this chamber specifically for her, as it was one of the most feminine in Misthaven with its white furnishings and match-

ing rose and leaf-green fabric at the windows and
bed. When they all arrived in the room, Colleen
gestured dramatically toward her velvet jewelry
case on the dressing table, then stood aside and
crossed one arm over the other as she prepared
to wait.

Harriet moved to the case without hesitation.
After looking through its drawers, she said, "I see
nothing here, but Colleen would be foolish to
store stolen goods in easy sight. Perhaps the dressing table . . ."

Roslyn could not allow this ridiculous scene to
continue. "Oh, let go, Harriet. We've invaded Colleen's privacy enough."

"No, no," said Colleen. "Search everything so
there won't be any questions later. Why don't
each of you take an item of furniture? It will be
quicker."

Roslyn had never seen Colleen look so bitter
or sad, and her emotions tumbled even further.
"I believe you, Colleen," she said. "I'm not touching anything."

"Nor am I," said Victoria.

"Well, I am." Harriet pulled out a drawer, its
screech sending shivers down Roslyn's spine.

"Colleen, dearest," Esther said, circling the
group to place an arm around Miss Sheridan's
waist. "Don't think for an instant that Harriet is
expressing *our* feelings. Naturally she's upset
about her pin, but she'll regain her composure
in a moment. I am so sorry."

"Well, I'm not!" Harriet lifted high a garnet

necklace. "Isn't this your missing pendant, Victoria?"

Victoria moved slowly to examine the jewelry. "Why, yes." Her shocked gaze settled on Colleen. "This is mine. The silver filigree is slightly tarnished, do you see? I'd meant to polish it."

"And this?" Harriet held aloft an opal ring.

"That belongs to me," Roslyn said, her voice thick with disbelief. "It was my mother's."

Colleen's eyes filled with tears. She stepped away from Esther. "I don't know how those got there. I don't. I swear to you, I didn't steal that jewelry!"

Less than a half hour later, the young ladies parted to return to their bedchambers. Roslyn entered her room feeling numb. She refused to believe that Colleen had stolen those items; her expressions of grief and shock had seemed too genuine. Someone must be playing a terrible trick, but who? Such an act was senseless.

Roslyn shivered as she recalled the distress of Colleen, who upon the discoveries had immediately declared she wanted to go home. Even Harriet had turned soothing at that point, refusing Colleen when she ripped the butterfly from her bodice and offered it to her, saying it must not be her pin after all; its eyes were red, not blue. During that moment, Roslyn felt kinder toward Harriet than she had all week.

When a further search of the room revealed no more of the missing pieces, the young ladies agreed upon one thing: to keep the matter secret for the time being. In this, Roslyn fibbed and felt sorry for it, but she knew she would seek the viscount's advice at the first opportunity.

After they had vowed their silence, Harriet again displayed unusual consideration when she spoke of reading a scientific article about people who performed strange acts in their sleep. Esther suggested that one of the servants might have mislaid the items.

Roslyn felt the latter idea to be far more likely, and so rang for Hetta. Some ten minutes later the servant arrived, by which time Roslyn was simmering.

"Why are you late so often, Hetta?" she demanded, knowing the answer would come as no surprise.

"I'm only one person," the servant said in aggrieved tones, "and I was helping Miss Pendergrass to change into her riding clothes."

This Roslyn didn't doubt for a moment, for so it had been from almost the moment Victoria entered the house. "Were you, indeed? And why were you helping her and not Miss Cummings or one of the other guests? More to the point, why didn't you answer *my* ring, since my father is the one employing you?"

Hetta's expression grew haughty. "That's not very nice. I thought you wanted to be kinder with us servants."

"I do mean to be kind, but not to the degree that you forget why you've been employed. It has, in fact, occurred to me that I never was unkind to you at all, even before my recent spot of madness when I went out of my way to treat you with consideration, and you responded by taking advantage of my patience. Now I'm telling you this: I wish things to return to normal."

Hetta sniffed. "That's as may be, but I'm only trying to guard my future."

"And what does that mean?"

"Only that you'll soon be a bride and will leave. I like this household. I've been at Misthaven forever, serving your mother before you. I've got friends here. I don't want to move miles away, no matter if Mr. Leffew would make a good master."

"Are you saying you don't wish to continue as my maid?"

"It's not that so much as I want to stay here." She walked to Roslyn's bed and smoothed a wrinkle from the coverlet. "And I've got eyes in my head. I can see how the land lies with Miss Pendergrass."

Roslyn became very still. "And just how *does* the land lie?"

"Everybody's been talking about it below stairs, but maybe I'd best not say more."

"Speak now or die," said Roslyn, her brows lowering.

"Well, all right." Hetta snickered. "But surely you know. Miss Pendergrass is always at your father's side and laps up his every word like a cat at cream. And he loves it. Any man would, a fine figure of a lady like that."

To have her fears confirmed so baldly almost

undid Roslyn. "Victoria is half my father's age," she reminded the servant in a deadly voice.

"Nothing strange about that. Happens all the time, older gentlemen marrying younger women, sometimes starting a new family."

A new family! This element had not yet occurred to her, and now she thought: *In a matter of a year or two, I could have siblings younger than my own children!* It was too much to contemplate, and only with difficulty did she subdue an impulse to run screaming from the room.

"Whatever lies in the future is anyone's guess," she declared. "For now, I'll thank you to remember you're *my* maid, and I expect you to act accordingly. Otherwise, you may find yourself without a position anywhere!"

"Yes, miss," Hetta said in humble tones, but her eyes sparkled avidly. Roslyn saw it with resignation. No doubt the servants would have a lively evening tonight with much to talk about.

Eleven

The rolling countryside of Hampshire was well known for its rural charm, and that afternoon Roslyn took a measure of peace from its familiar but beloved stretches of meadows and woodlands and flashes of river as she and her guests walked their horses down the lane. Unfortunately, that peace ran shallow, for her companions had magnified her distress fivefold. She could scarcely believe that ten days ago she had only her own problems over which to worry. Her project to marry off Lord Beaumont, so eagerly conceived and well-intentioned, had become a nightmare.

It had to be admitted the presence of young Miss Highton added to her distress, but at least that was none of Roslyn's doing. The prospect of Miles being trapped into marriage brought out her protective side, especially if there was trickery involved and Desiree was an imposter.

But weren't you doing the same—tricking him into joining your gathering in order to provide him with a bride? niggled an annoying voice.

No, she argued back. I wanted only the best for him.

Of course you did. That's why you invited one *lady you knew might please him. The other three were meant to cast yourself in a favorable light, so that he'd know what he missed in failing to marry you.*

"I'm shallow," she admitted to herself in a mumble. "I have a very small mind."

"What's that?" asked Miles, drawing Damon aside until she caught up with him. To her disappointment, Desiree also paused, with the result that the overgrown child now rode between them and made it necessary for Miles to lean forward and speak around her. "Are you talking to yourself, back here all alone?"

She *was* alone, she suddenly realized. Lost in her blue thoughts, she'd pulled ahead of Jonathan and Esther. Now she glanced over her shoulder and saw Jonathan helping her friend dismount to examine a garden fronting a cottage. She smiled as Esther bent to exclaim over a brilliant peony.

The riding party was much smaller than Roslyn had expected. Victoria, Harriet, and Colleen had decided to remain behind—each for their own reasons, Roslyn reflected dryly. Consequently their escorts had declined the outing, too, preferring to snore over newspapers in the library.

"I was only wishing I were more like your mother," Roslyn said, turning back to Miles.

"What, that again? You shouldn't want to be like anyone but yourself, which is a very good thing to be." Belatedly, he added, "Don't you agree, Desiree?"

The woman-child's eyes settled on Roslyn. "Yes,

although there's much to admire in the viscountess, particularly her work with the infirm. I shouldn't mind being like her, either."

"Why does everyone want to be like my mother?" he asked the clouds. "The truth is, I wish she'd take more time for herself. I constantly fear she'll contract a deadly disease in some hovel and leave us while she's still young enough to enjoy life—if she would only take the time."

To hear him express even such mild criticism of his sainted mother sent a glow through Roslyn, but she said, "At least she doesn't hatch idiotic schemes that do no one any good."

Miles sent her a smile around Desiree. "Now why would you say that, I wonder. Have you hatched an idiotic scheme recently?"

Roslyn bit her lip. "I was speaking in general terms."

"I see." He gave her a speculative look. "So you're reflecting on past sins—a worthy occupation for the Sabbath, I should imagine. Perhaps I can help you. Let me think . . . there are so many examples that I scarce know where to begin . . ."

Roslyn smiled ruefully, her gaze catching Desiree's. The girl's expression appeared sweet but lost—the look of one eager to travel but having no map. Roslyn could not help taking pity upon her, even if the child had won the world's dearest prize by default. Desiree was no more responsible for this disaster than Miles. In her own way, she, too, was a victim. If she was not a villainess, Roslyn amended to herself.

"Lord Beaumont has always enjoyed listing my sins, as he calls them," Roslyn confided, her heart growing light because of the viscount's jesting. He was falling back to their old sparring pattern, and she was grateful for the diversion, no matter how wistful it made her feel. "The list is so much shorter than his own, you see."

"Hah!" the viscount said. "We'll let Desiree judge between us, shall we? Just now I'm recalling the time when you tried to convince your father to purchase a puppy."

"That seems a reasonable request," Desiree ventured.

Roslyn lifted her brows at Miles. "There, you see?"

"Ah, but you don't know the whole story. Mr. Andrews detests animals that serve no purpose, in particular house dogs and cats. Pets make him sneeze and cough, and he declares they like to trip him."

"That only happened once," Roslyn said to Desiree. "When I was three years old, someone gave me the only pet I've ever owned—a kitten who loved him so much she wouldn't leave him alone."

"Mr. Andrews very nearly broke an arm falling over that cat. I recall him wearing a sling for almost a year."

"You recall no such thing; you were far too young to remember."

"My memory's not in question here; it's your

shady past we're discussing. The point is, Desiree, she well knew her father would refuse when she asked for the puppy. But she had an alternate plan."

"Miles, I'm certain Desiree has no interest in these old stories; you'll bore her to tears."

"No, I want to hear," Desiree said with a tentative smile, her head pivoting back and forth between them.

"I thought so, though you'll find the tale shocking," Miles declared. A sudden breeze began to ruffle the tops of the trees lining the road, and the viscount lifted his face to it, a mischievous expression in his eyes. "Roslyn pretended to become very ill. She refused all offers of food for days, though she had a secret stash in her bedroom and didn't suffer one pang of hunger. She used her mother's rice powder to appear pale and pathetic, and when her father called the physician, her acting skills were such that even the doctor believed her to be in failing strength, though he didn't know the cause. Only when Roslyn made her final request—an appeal for a furry companion to bring comfort to her last days—did Mr. Andrews become suspicious.

"To determine the truth, he made an offer. He would give her a dog if she was willing to sell her pony. He said that since she was so ill, she'd surely have no further need to ride." He laughed. "Roslyn experienced an immediate recovery, for there's nothing she likes better than trotting about the countryside."

Desiree remarked, "How clever of Mr. Andrews, though I wish he'd given you the dog, Roslyn."

The viscount batted away a dragonfly plaguing Damon's eyes. "I suppose he didn't want to encourage her naughtiness."

"*My* naughtiness?" Roslyn turned to Desiree. "How do you suppose I was able to eat during those days? It was Lord Beaumont who supplied my 'secret stash' of food. Every night he climbed in my window and provided me with supplies so that my servants didn't become suspicious, as they would have if I'd raided my own larder. He was my accomplice and bears the greater blame, since he's older and supposedly wiser."

"Your accomplice, indeed. I was simply trying to save you from starvation."

"How heroic you make yourself out to be. What you don't know, Desiree, is that his own schemes were far more devastating than mine."

Miles, his expression outraged, leaned forward in an exaggerated manner to gaze at Roslyn. "I beg your pardon. My youth was spent in an exemplary manner."

The laughter bubbling within Roslyn tasted delicious; it was the first real amusement she'd felt in days. "Would you name stealing timber to build a raft *exemplary?*"

"Stealing? That timber belonged to my estate."

"Yes, but your father intended to use it to build a prayer chapel for your mother."

"Perhaps, but no harm was done. The chapel exists, doesn't it?"

"Yes, though it required an additional year to

receive a new supply of that special redwood she wanted."

"Oh, look!" Desiree said suddenly, bringing Roslyn's attention back to her. "Those children are adorable." A set of dark-haired twins were tossing a ball back and forth in the front garden of a cottage. Between them, a smaller boy of about seven years tried to intercept the ball. "I should like to stop awhile and become acquainted. I love children."

"Of course," Miles said immediately. "The Albrights live here. They're a nice family; I'll introduce you."

"That's kind of you. And then you and Miss Andrews can continue your ride while I visit."

Miles look startled. "I wouldn't think of it. We'll wait, of course."

"No, no; I should feel awkward if you did."

The viscount regarded her a moment. "We *have* managed to bore you with our chatter about old times."

"Of course you haven't!" Desiree declared, with too much emphasis for total honesty, Roslyn believed. "But I confess I occasionally enjoy being with young ones. Maybe I'm still a child in some ways. I do know I'll feel *very* childish if the two of you wait while I play catch."

Roslyn, who could hardly believe her good fortune at the prospect of a few moments alone with the viscount, saw hesitation in his eyes. "Miles, if she truly wishes it, there are a few estate matters I need to discuss with you which I'm sure *would* bore Miss Highton."

"Oh, I'm sure, too," said Desiree, who swiftly added, "I'm sure I'd like to stay here while you discuss those matters, I mean."

With a shrug, Miles dismounted and helped Desiree from the saddle. Roslyn waited impatiently as he introduced her to the sweet-faced woman who came to the door, an infant at her hip. Desiree appeared to dissolve at the sight of the small one, and the compliments springing from her lips as she accepted the baby from Mrs. Albright made an immediate bond between the two women.

She is going to make Miles an excellent wife one day, Roslyn thought, her sadness returning.

"I wonder when Jonathan and Esther will catch up to us," Miles said as he climbed into the saddle.

"Not soon, I hope. I need your advice."

His mouth quirked into a smile. "On an estate matter, I believe you said. But aren't you a little worried about your guests?"

"If you're speaking of Esther, I know she's in good hands with Jonathan."

His eyes probed hers. "Aren't you at all concerned that they spend so much time together?"

"Why should I be?" she asked with a laugh. "They're very much alike in personality, I think, and so make good companions, and why I would mind that . . ." Her eyes widened. "Oh, Miles. You can't be thinking there's anything romantic between them. Why, how amusing! Jonathan is gallant toward Esther because of her trouble. That's simply the way he is."

The viscount said nothing, though his eyes expressed a thousand doubts. Roslyn couldn't like that, for she had admired his intelligence and perception since childhood. Was it possible Jonathan found Esther attractive in more than a casual way? If so, she pitied him. And Esther as well, if she felt the same, for there was not a thing they could do about it. Both were betrothed.

But if somehow Esther could wriggle free of Ames . . . would Jonathan want to be free from *her*?

No. He had too much honor to break off their engagement. Even she hadn't been willing to do that, and Roslyn was sure she possessed less virtue than Jonathan Leffew.

But if she was wrong . . .

A sudden vision of herself arose: Roslyn the spinster, growing ever more lonely, bitter, and wrinkled while Miles and Desiree raised a houseful of children across the road.

No!

She could not take on one more worry. Not today.

In indignant tones she said, "Why, only this morning in chapel, Jonathan held my hand."

"Oh, that answers it, then. All my suspicions are put to rest."

"I can see we don't agree, so please let's not talk about it anymore," Roslyn entreated. "Miles, I am in trouble."

The corners of his mouth lifted. "I would never have guessed it with you trailing behind everyone and talking to yourself. Has one of your *idiotic schemes* gone awry?"

After a second's debate, Roslyn decided to tell him; it couldn't matter now, and she had never liked to keep anything from Miles. Besides, her earlier thoughts about tricking him were plaguing her.

"Yes, as a matter of fact. This house party has brought . . . unexpected complications."

"Ah. I've wondered from the beginning why you wanted so many females to visit at one time. Wedding attendants they may be, but hosting so many for so long is begging for trouble."

"I did it for you."

For several long seconds, there were only the sounds of their horses' hooves meeting the road and the comfortable groanings of leather saddles. Northwind, irritable at the slow pace, tossed her head and snorted.

"If that's true, why did you do it?" Miles asked, finally. "You know how much I detest gatherings where practically everyone is a stranger."

"I wanted to help." Her courage, flaring so boldly only a moment ago, was deserting her now.

"Help? Do you believe I need lessons in extending my ability to tolerate tedium?"

"I thought you needed a bride," she said in a rush. "I didn't know at the time that you were betrothed, so I invited four of my closest friends to provide a selection for you. It seemed likely that one of them would attract your attention."

Miles pulled his steed to a complete stop. As soon as she realized it, Roslyn turned Northwind's head and joined him, but she found she had to force herself to return the viscount's fierce gaze.

When he spoke at last, she had the impression of one carefully restraining a fire. "And what gave you the notion that I needed a bride?"

"Because I was getting married," she said in a small voice, "and I didn't want you to be lonely."

The expression in his eyes softened. "You believed your marriage would make me lonely?"

She thought of answering him playfully, of reminding him of their long years of friendship and how she wanted him to be shackled like herself as a kind of revenge. In the end, she spoke the truth.

"Yes, and before you ask, it's because of the way you looked at me the night of my birthday ball," she said in a voice hardly more than a whisper. "When you left, you took my heart with you."

Roslyn nearly gasped at her own words. She hadn't meant to say anything so revealing, just as she hadn't dreamed tears would bubble to her eyes as she did.

Every vestige of anger dropped from the viscount's expression. To her surprised joy, he brought Damon closer, then reached out a hand to cup her cheek.

"And my heart remains with you," he said.

She closed her eyes. It was the closest he'd come to a declaration of his deepest feelings, and she wanted to savor the moment without worrying that at any second Jonathan, Esther, or Desiree might round the bend.

Slowly allowing her lashes to part, she knew that she could not, dare not, say anything further, but she covered his hand with hers and tried to put the thoughts of her heart into her eyes.

Northwind chose that moment to prance sideways, moving them apart. The spell broken, they laughed softly, Roslyn with regret.

"Your mare grows restless," Miles remarked.

"You know how she detests walking. Race me to the ruins?" she asked, naming a location some half-mile distant.

The horses bounded forward. Roslyn rejoiced in the burst of speed, the feel of wind tugging at the pins of her hat, the blur of a tunnel of trees stretching overhead, anything to prolong the intense ecstasy of the previous moments. Miles loved her. She had long hoped for it, though he'd never expressed the words. Now she knew. His eyes had told her. It was a bittersweet consolation to bring to her wedding with Jonathan, this tender memory they had made, but she would cherish it all her days.

Northwind and Damon were running neck and neck. The ruins, a decaying Roman bath well known to the locals, loomed ahead. Roslyn turned a blazing smile upon Miles and urged Northwind to go faster.

At that moment a hedgehog ran through the underbrush and across their path. Skittishly, Northwind danced closer to Damon and brushed his flank. When the black snorted his disapproval and nipped at her neck, the mare squealed and raised on hind legs. Roslyn shouted, tightened her legs, and leaned forward to keep her balance, but the sidesaddle provided poor support. She felt herself slipping as Northwind's forelegs thrashed the air.

Time suspended. Distantly she heard Miles commanding Northwind in soothing tones, and she thought he reached for her reins. There was a moment of blackness when she floated helplessly through the air; and she braced herself for a brutal landing, a landing that never came. When she opened her eyes, she found herself seated sideways across Damon, her cheek pressed against the viscount's waistcoat.

Miles was clutching her with fierce strength. She could feel the charging rhythm of his heart beneath her ear, hear the rapid sounds of his breath as he pulled her even closer.

When he asked her in a gruff voice if she was all right, she lifted her head and discovered his lips within a whisper of her own. His eyes, his beautiful clear eyes, had darkened to the grayish blue of wintry clouds. Without conscious thought, she threw her arms around his neck.

With the inevitability and grace of a dance that cannot be stopped, he brought his lips to hers, and sweet reluctance gave way to wild abandon. Though tears pricked her eyelids, she yielded gladly to his kisses, pressing herself closer to him, defying anything that might come between them, be it a breath of air, a wisp of light, or the promise of duty.

It was Miles who pulled back, making a sound between a groan and a sigh. "Forgive me," he whispered.

Fighting against thoughts of Jonathan, Desiree,

and all practicality, she nestled her head against his chest, her fingers lingering at his neck. She would allow nothing to spoil the perfection of the past moments, for it might be the only time in her life that she would recall with complete and total happiness.

"In my relief that you weren't hurt, I over-reacted," he added.

"I believe you saved me from a broken bone," she murmured contentedly to his shirt. "Thank you, Miles."

He was quiet for an instant. "I'm glad you understand. I would have tried to help anyone in your predicament, but if anything happened to you it would be a special tragedy. Since you'll soon be married, I mean. I couldn't allow you to proceed down the aisle in a wheelchair. You've been my friend and neighbor for as long as I can remember."

"All *right*, Miles," she said sharply, her hands falling to her lap.

"We're like family," he continued.

She viewed him through narrowed eyes. "Is that why you kissed me as you just did? If so, you have an unconventional manner with relatives, my lord, and I'd be failing our long association did I not inform you of it."

Slow lights began to move behind his eyes. "I thought *you* were kissing *me*." When her lips parted indignantly, he went on. "Because you were grateful."

It seemed he was determined to ruin the moment himself. "Yes, of course. Gratitude always brings such actions from me. You should see how I react when Marsden brings the mail."

Because she would not glance at him again, she sensed, rather than saw, his smile. "We'd better collect Northwind and find the others. They'll be wondering what happened to us."

"They won't be alone in their wondering," Roslyn grumbled.

On the journey back to collect Desiree, Miles spoke scarcely a word. He'd said enough, *done* enough, already. In yielding to his desire for Roslyn, he'd thrown her into further confusion and hurt. Not to mention himself. And no matter how he might try to pass off the past half hour as an aberration, there was no possible manner in which to mend things. Roslyn could see through him like glass.

When the Albright cottage came into sight, he tried to restore a semblance of normality by saying, "Did you mention something earlier about a problem?"

His heart constricted when she turned glassy eyes upon him. "I can't talk about that now."

"Of course. Maybe we can discuss it tonight after dinner." He sounded pathetically eager, but he wanted to atone for his behavior.

"I thought you were supposed to take Desiree to chapel for the evening service."

He groaned. "That's right; I'd forgotten."

By this time, Desiree had spotted them. Sitting on a stool in the garden, she still held the baby and had apparently spent the past moments chatting with Mrs. Albright as they watched the children play. Now she rose and returned the infant to its mother. While Miles helped Desiree settle into her saddle, she bid cheerful good-byes to her new acquaintances.

"I'm surprised Jonathan and Miss Cummings haven't caught up with us yet," Miles remarked as they turned their horses homeward. To Desiree, he added, "You haven't seen them?"

"No, but they might have ridden past when I wasn't looking. We went inside a little while for a glass of milk."

Miles felt Roslyn's gaze upon him and determined to say no more, though he felt uneasy. Unconventional behavior was unlike Leffew. Miles couldn't imagine him leading Esther off the path for a few moments alone, no matter how strong the romantic pull. But love could make idiots of men; hence his own behavior this afternoon.

"We would have passed them if that were the case," Roslyn said woodenly, her gaze directed on the path ahead. "Esther may have felt unwell, and Jonathan took her home."

"That's the likeliest explanation," Miles acknowledged, although he didn't believe it for an instant. The last time he'd looked, Esther had appeared in the best of health, even seemed to *glow* as she conversed with Jonathan.

A silence descended. It was not a comfortable one, at least not for him. Roslyn's unhappiness magnified his own tenfold.

He searched his mind for alternatives to their

situation, alternatives that would make it possible for him to spend the remainder of his days with Roslyn.

He could break off with Desiree and abandon the estate in which generations of Beaumonts had lived. Then he would have to find employment. He was not too proud to work for his living. London would be the best choice for that.

But the prospect of moving Roslyn and his mother to the kind of gloomy, unsafe neighborhoods he'd be able to afford made the blood freeze in his veins. And there was the promise he'd made to his father to consider. He was to retain his family's honor at all cost.

There was no solution that would bring happiness. The love he and Roslyn shared would not be the first to be sacrificed on the altar of duty, he supposed. It was a pity that knowledge didn't lighten the pain.

He glanced at Desiree, who was staring ahead with a characteristic half smile. A pretty girl, but so strange in her silences. She had not volunteered one comment after leaving the Albright cottage. It seemed to him that a young woman professing such an interest in children as she had would now be brimming over with stories about how adorable the Albright children were or some such feminine nonsense. Instead she remained as quiet as if she'd never visited.

Perhaps she was shy, though he doubted it. Maybe her head was full of doubts about their alliance. He should make more of an effort to charm her, but he couldn't. He would do his duty and nothing more. If she decided against him, so be it.

As if fleeing his thoughts, Desiree allowed her horse to pull ahead to the top of the next rise. She appeared an excellent rider, so when she drew her mount to a sudden stop, he felt immediate alarm.

"Mr. Leffew's horse," she said, as he and Roslyn trotted forward.

He looked from her concerned eyes to the path ahead, which was a lonely, wooded stretch that ran for a few acres between cottages. Jonathan's gray was nibbling at the grass. There was no sign of Leffew or Esther.

"Wait here," Miles commanded the ladies, and urged Damon on. Something was definitely wrong, and he didn't believe it could be so simple as a romantic tryst or Esther's beast would be nearby.

As he drew near the abandoned horse, he heard hoofbeats behind him and turned to see Roslyn approaching. He should have known she would do as she pleased. At least Desiree had listened to him; she waited at the crest of the hill, though her steed pranced back and forth as if feeling his mistress's uncertainty.

"Go back, Roslyn," he said. "There may be danger."

"I saw something," she told him as she cantered past. Exasperated, he pressed Damon to follow Roslyn, whose back was stiff with tension. She rode beyond the gray to a thicket about a quarter mile distant. By the time she slid from the saddle, he, too, had spotted the body half-hidden in a stand of gorse. He dismounted at a run, his heart pounding.

"Jonathan!" Roslyn cried, kneeling beside the motionless form. "Is he dead, Miles? Oh, please don't tell me he's dead!"

"He's not dead, my love. Calm yourself." The viscount checked for broken bones, then gently turned Jonathan to his side. As he did, he discovered a cut at the back of Leffew's head. "Here. Looks as though he struck his head on something when he fell."

"Struck his head on what? There aren't any rocks or hard objects here! And where is Esther? Do you think she rode home for help?"

Miles shook his head to express his unwillingness to guess, then lightly tapped Jonathan's cheek, trying to awaken him. Roslyn sat back on her heels, her eyes wide and solemn. He hoped she wasn't thinking the same thoughts that were firing through his brain.

"Wake up, Jonathan," she begged. "You must wake up and tell us where Esther is. *Where is Esther?*"

Leffew's lids quivered open. Glazed eyes moved from Miles to Roslyn in hazy contemplation, then sudden awareness.

"Roslyn," he whispered. "So . . . sorry. Unforgivable . . . Didn't see him . . ."

"See *who*? Jonathan—"

"Ames," he breathed. "Ames has her."

Twelve

"Which way did they go?" Roslyn cried. "Miles, we must find her!"

"Steady, Roslyn," the viscount said, helping Jonathan to stand. "First we need to see that Jonathan gets to Misthaven safely."

Jonathan stepped away from Miles. "No, she's right. Go after Esther . . . I'll be fine." His knees began to fold, and the viscount hurried to steady him. "You must . . . hurry."

"Yes, hurry you home, if you think you can keep your seat."

When Jonathan declared he could, Miles began to assist him toward his horse. Roslyn hurried to his other side, supporting her injured fiancé as best she could. His pale skin and obvious pain pricked her heart, and she felt sorry for seeming to be concerned only for Esther. Still, she could scream with impatience. Every passing second took her friend farther away.

By this time, Desiree had joined them, and the foursome slowly made their way back to Misthaven while Jonathan haltingly told them what had happened: After he and Esther finished exploring the garden where Roslyn had last seen them, they had remounted with the intention of joining the others. They rode only a short way before Braxton Ames overtook them, seemingly appearing from nowhere.

"Though he must have been trailing us all morning, waiting for such an opportunity as this," Jonathan added. "If I hadn't encouraged Miss Cummings to view the flowers, he wouldn't have been able to abduct her so easily. I blame myself."

"Nonsense." Miles scanned the sky ahead, a slight frown on his brow. "If he was that intent on taking her, he would have done so anyway. Much as it pains me to say so, we must consider that he has her father's permission to return Esther home."

Roslyn could not believe her ears. "Miles, how can you say such a thing? We don't know for certain he has her father's permission; we have only Braxton Ames's word for it." She knew the argument was weak, for her friend's father seemed a cold, demanding creature who cared little for his daughter's wishes. (Roslyn had never set eyes upon him, but not once had he allowed Esther to visit her at Misthaven during their school days, and she needed no greater proof than that.) "Besides, why would he harm Jonathan if his intentions are so noble?"

"He knew it was the only way he could get her away from me," Jonathan said, sounding so fierce that Roslyn gazed at him in surprise. "When he demanded that Esther go with him, she reminded him he'd promised she could stay the week. He

said he had business to attend to, and that the
delay was frivolous and a waste of his time. I saw
how determined he was, so I grabbed Esther's
reins and turned back in time to see his arm descending with the barrel of his blunderbuss
pointed at me. I didn't react quickly enough. I
hadn't anticipated sudden violence."

"Or such a cowardly act," Roslyn said. "To
strike when you weren't looking."

"That *was* unfair of him," said Desiree, drawing
Roslyn's startled eyes. She had almost forgotten
the girl was with them. "Poor Miss Cummings."

Jonathan took little comfort from their words.
"I don't even know in which direction they left.
It's my fault she's gone."

"No, Jonathan," Roslyn said, although her
heart was breaking that he hadn't been able to
save her. "Don't blame yourself; you couldn't
know. But we must rescue her." She turned to
Miles. "You do see that, don't you? Braxton is a
violent man, and Esther is very afraid of him."

"He's probably taking her back to Essex," Miles
said.

Roslyn had no difficulty imagining the worst.
"Unless he's running away with her to Gretna
Green."

"No need for that, not if Esther's father is
agreeable to the wedding."

The viscount's voice was mild, and he appeared
unable to look directly at her; he persisted in
looking into the distance as if trying to spot a
hawk. If this was how he intended to behave after

kissing her so passionately, he would drive her mad.

"There's no imagining what a beast like him will do," Roslyn said finally, "but you're probably right. Essex at least gives us a direction. There might be time to overtake them before they arrive home."

Miles gave her a look colored with compassion. "I've no objection to trying to find Esther, but we'll simply be postponing the inevitable."

"She can't marry him, Miles! Her life will be destroyed. Someone must talk with her father."

"What would that avail, if he's as hard a man as I've been led to believe?"

"He can't *force* her to wed him, can he? She's an adult. If she has nothing to live on, then—then she can live with me. Although Father wouldn't like having his privacy invaded . . ." She turned to Jonathan. "Could she stay with us after we're married?"

Leffew hesitated only an instant before saying, "Of course."

At least this interchange appeared to capture the viscount's attention. He gave her an intent, troubled look, then returned his gaze to the sky ahead.

"What could possibly be wrong with that?" Roslyn asked him, although she knew what he was thinking. He believed Jonathan had a *tendre* for Esther and that having her under the same roof would not be the best thing for their marriage. But *she* didn't believe in the alleged attraction for a moment. Jonathan was naturally kind—kind to *everyone*.

"Esther is the most agreeable of companions," she added. *And would be a comfort to me,* she almost continued, but stopped herself in time. Jonathan might wonder why his bride-to-be felt she needed comforting. "Don't you agree, Miles, that this would be the best solution?" She could not let him alone; something within her craved his approval. After a long silence, she said in vexation, "Why will you not look at me? Am I boring you?"

Miles did not react to her statement. If anything, his gaze sharpened on the horizon. Following his line of vision, she suddenly realized what had been occupying his attention.

"Fire!" she cried.

There could be no doubting the source of the flames. The riding party was topping the last hill that led downward to Misthaven, and the hungry tongues of fire bellowing upward were too near, too violent, to be anything but a burning structure on the Andrews estate.

Roslyn pressed Northwind forward. Her home couldn't be on fire. Her entire life was centered there. Every corner, every wall, every stick of furniture spurred a memory of times that would never come again. The brocade chair in her sitting room immediately came to mind; when memory grew dim of her mother, Roslyn had only to look at it to recall being held in her lap and hearing stories. Oh, and the paintings of their family; they were irreplaceable. This simply could not be happening. Fires brought utter destruction. Fires brought death.

Please, God, keep my father and the others safe.

Arriving at the summit, she heaved a great sigh of relief. The stable was engulfed, yes, but the house was untouched. Her relief dissipated as she saw the frantic lines of people scurrying to put out the fire. It was apparent the concern uppermost in everyone's mind was keeping the house safe.

Every servant and guest appeared to be in the yard, some running with buckets of water, others stamping out stray flames, still others trying to tether the horses, which were wild in their fear. Thank God the horses had been saved!

Less felicitous was the reigning panic and disorder; though her father shouted out commands, Roslyn knew the safety of the house was in serious jeopardy.

She registered all of this in the seconds it took her to gallop into the stable yard with Miles at her side and Desiree and Jonathan close behind. The viscount tossed off his jacket and immediately began to assist her father in organizing the workers. Between them, they managed to arrange an organized line of bucket carriers between pump and stable. Roslyn took her place in line, as did Desiree and Jonathan, even though she begged him to rest because of his injury.

Once the workers were set in place, Miles seized a shovel and joined the strongest men in driving back the fire. He was working harder than anyone, Roslyn saw, too numbed with shock to feel

anything but concern that he'd chosen the most
dangerous task and fought far too closely to the
fire.

Amid the shouts and cries, Roslyn became
aware of one voice sounding shrilly over the others.

"Mr. Crim! Mr. Crim!" shouted Harriet Pollehn,
running back and forth in front of the burning
stable. "Has anyone seen Mr. Crim?"

A section of roof looked ready to give way, and
Harriet stood dangerously near it as she scanned
the crowd. Fearing for her friend's safety, Roslyn
broke from the line and sped to her.

"Get back, Harriet!" she cried, then swept her
arm around the young woman's shoulders and
tried to tug her toward safety.

"But Mr. Crim!" she exclaimed, resisting. "My
cats!"

Roslyn's spirits sank at the thought of Roger
Crim being caught in the blaze. She had known
the faithful groom since childhood, when he had
begun as a stable boy. He was not overly bright,
but he was a good and kind man.

"Oh, my dear, perhaps he and your cats are
safe—"

"But the cats were trapped in cages! Only
Three knew how to unlock them quickly, and he's
gone!"

"There's nothing that can be done now," Roslyn said, pulling. "Come, Harriet."

"Roslyn, the roof!" called Miles. He was racing
toward them. Taking warning from his urgent ex-

pression, Roslyn did not pause to gaze behind her, but jerked Harriet's arm and ran.

The sound of falling timbers brought her heart to her throat. A wave of heat seared toward them. Panic darkened the edges of her vision, and for a moment she thought she might faint. And then Miles was there, patting out the embers that had landed on the back of her skirt, then doing the same for Harriet.

"Are you all right?" he demanded of Roslyn, and when she nodded, seized her in a brief embrace. "Stay out of harm's way, will you? Leave the heroism for me."

"I d-don't have time to w-wait for that," she said, trying to return his attempt at lightness.

"Well, take the time, do you hear?" He brushed a strand of hair from her eyes. "I couldn't bear it if you were harmed." With his thumb he rubbed a circle on her forehead, then kissed the spot. "You're black as a cook pot."

He raced back to his work. Roslyn persuaded Harriet to join the line of sweating helpers. This was not the time to mourn; not yet.

She could see the stable was a total loss. The prospect of further destruction was alarming enough, but even if nothing was threatened, neither property damage nor bodily harm, the force of the blaze alone shook her with its frightening power. As she passed bucket after bucket, her arms beginning to protest, she watched the blaze with horrified awe. The fire appeared to be a living creature. She could almost believe the flames *sang* as the inferno thrust its greedy arms upward in joyous destruction.

She would consign the stable to the fire. The creature had won that. But no more, no more; no sacrifices of human flesh, and not her home. Yet as the minutes stretched to an hour and more, Roslyn felt how pitiable were their efforts against such an elemental force. Tears ran pathways down her sooty cheeks. The heat was worse than anything she had ever known.

It was the arrival of their neighbors that turned the battle. The viscount's household was first to come, Lady Beaumont leading the procession. While she and Mrs. Highton distributed dozens of sandwiches, the viscount's servants joined the effort. Soon scores of people arrived from nearby cottages and estates to help.

It touched her to know how much her neighbors cared. At least the tragedy had brought that.

After many hours the fire gave way, burning down to a smoldering presence that could be managed by the male servants in watches during the night. The neighbors gradually drifted away.

As sunset yielded to the dark, a few of the house guests who had not yet gone inside gathered at the kitchen gate and stared wearily at the destruction. Harriet was one, though she stood a short distance away from the others and gazed at the ruined stable with desolate eyes. Roslyn was moving toward her when her father's words stilled her.

"Fifty years and never a fire till now," he said, propping one arm on the stone wall sheltering the kitchen garden. Beneath the soot, he looked so pale and tired that Roslyn feared for him. "I don't know why it happened now. Without Roger we may never know."

"Oh," sobbed Harriet, as if struck.

"Go inside, Father, and rest," Roslyn said. "You, too, Harriet . . . Desiree. I suppose that's what we should all do." She looked pointedly at the viscount, then downward to Jonathan, who sat with his back against the stones, his head tilted backward and eyes closed. "Some of us need to rise early to go in search of Esther." The fire, harrowing as it had been, had not driven her friend's danger from her mind for a moment.

"Esther . . ." echoed her father. "But she's gone back to her home with that Ames fellow."

"How did you know that?" Roslyn said sharply.

"Why, they came to collect her belongings shortly before you returned."

"And Esther mentioned nothing about how she came to be with him?" Roslyn could not believe it. "She didn't say he struck Jonathan and stole her away?"

Mr. Andrews's eyes grew round. "No. Did he? Are you all right, Jonathan? Did you strike him back and show him how the land lies?"

Without opening his, Leffew said bitterly, "I went out . . . like a swooning girl."

"Oh." Roslyn's father looked so disappointed that she would have laughed had the circumstances not been so grim. "Well, I'm sure you did your best. How odd that she said nothing about it. But come to think upon it, she looked white as a specter the whole time, and he didn't let her out of his sight. Even went with her as she packed."

"Did the fire begin before they left or after?" Miles asked.

The silence was thick as they all turned to Mr. Andrews. A look of dead certainty came into his eyes. "Some five minutes after he took her from the house."

"We have our arsonist," Jonathan said. "What better way to prevent us from following immediately than to start a fire?"

"Oh, Esther," Roslyn breathed. "I wonder if he means to marry her as soon as they return."

"But that makes no sense," Mr. Andrews said. "Roslyn, the last thing she said was for me to tell you it's for the best, that she'd decided she wanted to marry him after all."

Roslyn was struck silent for the length of several heartbeats. "She couldn't have meant it." Her gaze fell to Jonathan; and suddenly, she thought she knew why Esther had lied.

Jonathan said, "Ames knew we wouldn't believe she'd changed her mind, or he wouldn't have set the fire."

"We don't know he did." Mr. Andrews crossed his arms. "Maybe those idiot cats set it. They could do everything else."

Even as Harriet's voice raised in protest, Roger Crim rounded the garden gate clutching three struggling felines in his arms. "Watch what you say about these cats, Master Thurmond," he said. "They saved my life."

Thirteen

"My darlings!" squealed Harriet, running forward and taking two of the felines. "Oh, Mr. Crim, thank you, and it's so good to see you survived. To have One, Two, and Four back—what joy! But—not that I mean to sound ungrateful, Mr. Crim—but are these the only ones who escaped?"

Left with the easier burden of a single feline, Roger beamed. "These were the only ones I could catch, miss. I been in the woods looking ever since the fire started and they woke me."

"You were searching for cats while the rest of us were working like slaves to prevent my house burning down?" Mr. Andrews said in outrage, but Roslyn tugged his hand and gave him a look that begged for silence.

"Well, I thought I owed it to them, sir," Roger said. "I was taking my Sunday afternoon nap when I heard a terrible howling going on. I got off my bed and went to the ladder. The fire was going strong at the north end. I saw a stranger running away. My first thought was for the horses, so I hurried down and got them out. Then I went back for the cats, because they was what woke me, and because Miss Pollehn is so fond of them."

"Oh, bless you!" Harriet cried.

Roger's ruddy cheeks darkened further. "Well, don't give me too much thanks, miss. The smoke was so bad I couldn't get back in. It was Three what got them out."

"Three?" Harriet's chin lifted. Her eyes shone with instant pride.

"Yes, miss. He went in and got them loose, one after the other. I stood watching like a stick, because I couldn't believe my eyes. In and out, in and out he went. When they was all free, off to the woods they ran."

"Oh, *my!*" said Harriet.

Roslyn couldn't help smiling at the wobble in the young woman's voice. Truly the feat *was* amazing. She wished she could have seen it.

"So I followed them and caught what I could."

Mr. Andrews's face was still etched in a frown. "If you felt you had to go hunting, you could have at least alerted the household that there was a fire."

"Oh, by that time everybody was running out," Roger assured him.

Miles remarked, "You said you saw a man leaving the stable. What did he look like?"

"Dressed like a gentleman he was, milord, though I won't call him one. I think he was here last night, though he didn't put his horse in the stable. I saw him leave when I was out walking."

"Then it *must* have been Mr. Ames who set the fire," Desiree said, the disappointment in her voice surprising Roslyn. "I hoped it was caused by an accident. I detest knowing people are capable of such acts."

Roslyn could not help staring. Truly, the longer she knew the child, the odder she seemed. But that was ungenerous; Desiree had worked as valiantly as anyone in their struggle this afternoon, and her dark gown, now stained and torn, looked to be a total loss. Desiree didn't appear to mind. She seemed to lack vanity.

Desiree *would* make Miles a fine wife. Roslyn wanted to hate her for it, especially now that certain terrible thoughts were circling through her brain, thoughts clamoring for a decision. But she couldn't hate the quiet child. She didn't even believe Desiree was an imposter any longer. That had only been wishful thinking on her part anyway. She felt certain the viscount's inquiries would lead to nothing.

With reluctance she lowered her gaze to Jonathan. He was looking into the distance, his eyes bleak. His posture bespoke a weariness that went beyond the physical.

She glanced away and found the viscount watching her. His smile was sweet, wistful. Roslyn longed to walk into his embrace, feel his strong arms around her again.

The kitchen door opened, and Victoria came out. She had bathed the dirt and scent of fire from her skin and dressed in an ivory gown. Clean, damp hair hung in waves across her shoulders and halfway down her back. She looked like a goddess standing at the top of the shallow stairs, a goddess descending to smile gracefully at her smudge-faced minions leaning against the wall.

But this goddess had pleaded faintness after less than an hour of passing pails and gone inside. *Her* energy had been spent restoring her glorious image.

Roslyn's lip curled. Here was one person she believed she *could* hate, especially when she noted how her father's eyes brightened as he looked at Victoria.

"Might I persuade all of you to come inside?" Victoria asked. "I've taken the liberty of having the servants boil water for baths." She shot a nervous look at Roslyn. "I hope you don't mind, but all of you were so busy with the fire that someone needed to see to it, so I pulled a few of the servants inside once everything seemed under control. Cook is preparing a simple meal for us, and it should be ready by the time you've finished dressing."

"I've never heard sweeter words," Mr. Andrews said. "Come in, all of you. No sense in tarrying to view the damage. Don't worry over what can't be fixed." As Roslyn grudgingly moved to the door, he patted her back and whispered, "Besides, the expense isn't our worry now but Jonathan's. Good thing we're getting him in the family, what? And not a moment too soon!"

Her father's words echoed in Roslyn's ears as she luxuriated in her hip bath behind the screen in her bedchamber. Sliding a soap-filled cloth over her arms and legs, she tried to banish the sound of his voice by concentrating on how good the warm water felt. Nothing worked, not even submerging her head beneath the bubbles.

Her father could not have said anything worse. Not given the tenor of her most recent thoughts.

Still, she had made up her mind. Or believed she had.

She felt like a small bird struggling against a powerful wind that tossed her first in one direction, then the other.

She was draping herself in a thick robe when a frantic knocking sounded. Recognizing Colleen's voice, Roslyn wrapped her hair in a towel and opened the door.

"It is beyond belief what I've found," Colleen said, marching into the room without preamble. The light in her eyes was intense, almost feverish.

Eyeing Colleen's well-dressed appearance, Roslyn realized she had not seen the young woman all afternoon. Although she knew it went beyond the bounds of hospitality to demand help from her guests during an emergency, she couldn't prevent herself from expecting them to offer.

"Were you aware that our stable burned down today?" she asked, taking care to keep her tone neutral.

"La, Roslyn, have pity and don't fault me for not throwing water on the fire. I looked out the window and saw my feeble help would make no difference, so I took advantage of the diversion to search rooms. No one accuses *me* of stealing!

It was a good thing I did, too. Look what I found in Harriet's room—my pearl necklace!"

Roslyn examined the proffered pearls, then scanned her guest's face. "In Harriet's room, you say?"

"I know what you're thinking—that I put it there. I knew everyone would be suspicious of me after Harriet's accusation, and it's terribly unjust! Why don't we confront her and see what she says? She has other jewels in her box that I wondered about, too."

Colleen's expression brooked no denial, so Roslyn put on her slippers and followed her to Harriet's room. If Colleen had planted the jewelry, she must be deeply disturbed to think anyone would believe her on her word alone. On the other hand, if *Harriet* had stolen the jewels, she was hardly likely to confess.

She would never have a house party again, not so long as she lived.

Harriet opened the door cradling one of the cats over her shoulder. She started guiltily at the sight of Roslyn, then raised her head, her expression growing defiant.

"It can't be helped," she said.

"There, you see!" crowed Colleen. "She admits it already!"

Harriet looked confused, then frowned. "There's no other place to put them. Besides, they're heroes; you heard Roger—Mr. Crim, I mean. Mr. Andrews can surely have no objection."

"You're mad," Colleen said, her voice suddenly subdued.

Roslyn sighed. "This is not about the cats, Harriet. May we come in?"

Harriet stepped back to admit them. As Roslyn was crossing the threshold, she caught sight of Victoria in the corridor. She forced her face into a pleasant mask and reminded herself that only one week remained before her guests would go home.

"Roslyn, I was just coming to fetch you. Your father says to hurry, they're all famished." Victoria's brows lifted curiously as she stared into the doorway.

"Good," Colleen said, grabbing her arm. "You come inside, too, and serve as another witness."

"Witness to what?" Harriet said.

"This!" Colleen thrust forward her necklace.

The yellow cat suddenly pounced on Roslyn's slippers. She was so busy trying to avoid him that she almost missed the expressions crossing Harriet's face.

"Oh." Harriet stepped back, then sat on the bed.

"You don't—" Roslyn, a look of distaste in her eyes, gently nudged the feline away with her foot—"deny it?"

Harriet began to stroke her cat faster. "Well . . ."

Only this morning Harriet had made a scene accusing Colleen. Roslyn struggled to comprehend this new turn of events, and found she could not. Had Harriet been trying to divert attention from herself? But such a thing was unnecessary; to her knowledge, no one had suspected

Harriet. By pointing her finger at Colleen, she had made matters worse.

"Are you responsible for all the thefts?" Roslyn demanded, still trying to sort through her confusion.

"I didn't *steal* the jewelry," Harriet said primly. "I borrowed it."

Victoria stepped closely to Harriet. "If you borrowed it, then why did you make everyone think Colleen was a thief?"

"That's what I want to know," Colleen said, also drawing nearer.

Harriet's stroking of her cat became so rapid that her victim growled and wriggled away. "It was all part of the experiment."

"Experiment!" cried three young voices at once.

"Yes. I wanted to see how you would behave once your jewelry went missing. I hypothesized that you would begin to suspect each other once the servants were ruled out, and I wanted to see which personality type garnered the most suspicion, whether laughing Colleen, compliant Victoria, sweet Esther, or brave Roslyn."

In the middle of her outrage, Roslyn's interest was piqued. "You think I'm brave?"

Harriet shrugged. "You saved my life this afternoon. Before that, I thought of you as tempestuous Roslyn."

"Tempestuous . . ." Roslyn murmured, not sure she liked the term.

"What difference does it make what she calls us?" Colleen cried. "How dare you stage this embarrassing episode today, Harriet! You destroyed me!"

"Bosh. You're not destroyed. I had to accuse somebody, because no one was reacting, or if you were, you kept boringly quiet about it. So I began with the butterfly brooch. Later this week, when everyone suspected Colleen, I planned to slip other pieces of jewelry into additional rooms. Esther's pendant"—she went to her dresser and pulled out a gold locket—"would be left in Roslyn's chamber. I hoped to leave it in an obvious place where Roslyn would see it. Then if she remained quiet, it would reveal a larcenous side to her character, do you see? And Mr. Andrews's watch is already resting in Victoria's case; I suppose she hasn't noticed it yet. From your responses, I could gain valuable knowledge about how people react when under unusual and stressful situations."

"You should be locked up and the key thrown away," Victoria said baldly, and for once Roslyn agreed with her.

"It's the scientific method," Harriet said, scanning their faces with a look of appeal. "I don't expect you to understand."

"You're the worst person I've ever known," Colleen said.

Harriet raised her chin haughtily, though her eyes flickered with hurt. "Genius is never recognized in its own time. I won't stand for more of your insults. First thing tomorrow, I'm going home!"

"Harriet—" Roslyn began.

"I think it's for the best," Victoria told Roslyn. "When your father finds out she stole his watch . . ."

Colleen's nose wrinkled. "Yes, do go home, Harriet, even if it means I must ride the mail coach back. But you're not leaving before you tell Ned and Gregory—all the others, I mean—the truth."

At Oakwood Castle, Miles rose from his bath—the fastest one he could ever recall taking—and briskly rubbed himself down with a towel. He dressed rapidly, grimacing at his reflection in the mirror when his cravat refused to knot properly and wishing he had not found it necessary to dismiss his valet as a measure of economy.

Had it not been for his growing desire to be near Roslyn at every possible moment, he would have acceded to his mother's request that he remain at Oakwood for dinner tonight. But when Thurmond Andrews's gratitude for their actions during the fire led him to invite Miles's family to supper, the viscount could not refuse, though the older ladies declared themselves too tired. Thus he prepared to return to Misthaven alone.

When he entered the library to bid the ladies farewell, he was surprised to find Desiree wished to go with him. She looked fresh as a spring flower despite her mourning gown, and he could not refuse her. He ordered the gig, and within moments they set out.

At first she was quiet as usual. Her long silences

increasingly bothered him. He wasn't sure why. Perhaps it was because he suspected much was going on behind that sweet facade she presented to the world. He had no clue as to what it might be, but he was certain her quiet manner had nothing to do with a sluggish mind.

After Miles had inquired after her health and offered the usual pleasantries, Desiree finally said something on her own.

"When do you plan to search for Miss Cummings?" she asked.

Thinking of the coming day, he sighed. He wanted to help Esther in any way possible, but he didn't have hope the matter would be resolved quite so easily as Roslyn believed.

"At first light, probably, though nothing has been decided. We'll discuss it tonight."

"Miss Andrews will accompany you and Mr. Leffew?"

Miles gave a short laugh. "No doubt she'll try. I plan to discourage her, as the situation is likely to be unpleasant."

"If she does accompany you, I'd like to go as well."

He was silent a moment, pretending to be involved with turning the mare onto the road. "Would you? I imagine your mother would have something to say about that."

"She has already given me permission, if you will allow it."

"Why? Why would you want to go with us? As I said, it's bound to be unpleasant."

"I'm not a stranger to unpleasantness, Lord

Beaumont. Miss Cummings's plight troubles me. If I can help in any way, I want to do so."

He stared and murmured noncommitally. He was used to young girls chattering about clothes and balls, not assisting people they barely knew. Was she genuine, or was there something hidden behind her innocent mask? And what did she mean by not being a stranger to unpleasantness?

She was a puzzle, but not one he sought to solve. Roslyn owned his heart, and she wouldn't let go; that much was certain, or he'd be at Oakwood soaking his sore muscles instead of parking the gig in front of Misthaven after dark.

However, when Marsden opened the door to admit the viscount and his companion, Miles immediately realized he should have remained at home. Loud, angry voices could be heard in the parlor, and the tension in the house was palpable as heat.

Exchanging a worried look with Desiree, he led her cautiously forward; but before they reached the doorway, Harriet Pollehn rushed from the room, brushed past them without meeting their eyes, and dashed up the stairs. Before he could react, Desiree excused herself and followed.

With a sense of one entering a play after the second act is halfway through, he strode into the parlor and was soon apprised of Miss Pollehn's actions by an irate Mr. Andrews.

"Offer the girl hospitality, even put up with her wild animals, and this is the thanks I get," he concluded. "Well, she's leaving tomorrow, so that's that. Dinner's ready, and I'm not waiting another minute."

Roslyn, looking so radiant in her rose gown that Miles wanted to devour her, said, "I think I saw Miss Highton going up the stairs."

"She'll forgive us for dining without her," her father said. "If we don't eat, I'll starve."

The company retired to the dining room, Miles offering his arm to Roslyn before Jonathan had risen from his chair. The viscount felt no guilt in doing so. Jonathan would have the rest of his life to act as her escort. By his glum look, he was beyond caring, anyway. Still angry at himself for losing Esther, Miles imagined. Maybe his wound hurt.

"Your Miss Pollehn is a woman of many surprises," Miles said to Roslyn after the first course had been served. Her arms were bare to her puffed sleeves. He wanted to move his fingers slowly across her smooth skin, to kiss the tender flesh inside her elbows. Madness. Fortunately Desiree chose that moment to enter the room, and was led by Marsden to the empty chair between Gregory and Mr. Andrews, thus restoring his sanity.

"I feel sorry for her," Roslyn was saying, "but she was very wrong to do what she did."

He lowered his voice for her ears alone. "Yes, and had it been left to you, I might have chosen her for a bride. Are all of your selected prospects so larcenous?"

Her smile delighted him. It did not appear to have the same effect upon Jonathan. Clattering his spoon into his bowl of soup, he stood abruptly, his solemn gaze moving between them, then settling upon Roslyn. For one tense second Miles thought he'd perceived the truth about them.

"You must excuse me," said Jonathan. "While some of you appear to be able to laugh and chat as though this were a normal situation, I cannot— not while Miss Cummings is suffering."

Beneath the table, Roslyn's hand clutched the viscount's arm in what he believed to be shock, perhaps even guilt. Her eyes flooded with desolation. Miles longed to strike Leffew for his breach of manners.

"We're all concerned about Miss Cummings's situation," said the viscount, "but after becoming acquainted with her for these few days, I believe her character is such that she wouldn't want her friends denying themselves food and a good night's sleep before coming to her aid."

"Miss Cummings is a frightened young woman without a protector. You didn't see the terror that came into her eyes when Ames approached us. I can't sit in comfort any longer—not while she's with that scoundrel."

Roslyn began to cry softly. Miles swept an arm around her shoulders and offered his handkerchief. Face flushing, he turned on Leffew. "Are you pleased with yourself?"

Jonathan lowered his head. "I have no wish to hurt Roslyn, but I'm going after Miss Cummings. Now."

At this, Ned Leffew scraped back his chair. "You'll do no such thing, Brother. You're shaking like an old woman. What good will you do anyone falling into a ditch?"

Mr. Andrews, no fool he, was regarding his future son-in-law with alarm. "Right, right. You'd best not go at all, given that blow you took to the head. Leave it to the others."

"There's no moon tonight," Miles said, not without compassion, for it was obvious how deeply Jonathan's feelings ran for the girl—even deeper than the viscount had suspected. Had it been Roslyn in Ames's possession, nothing could have stopped him from following. "We'll serve Esther better after resting and save the horses from stumbling in the dark as well. If we leave early enough, we can make Essex long before nightfall."

Jonathan's eyes locked with his. With pity Miles sensed his struggle, though he dreaded to think what it portended for Roslyn's future.

"Very well, then," Jonathan said at last. "We'll depart before dawn and pray it's not too late."

Fourteen

Sunrise was at least an hour away when the viscount's coach turned onto Misthaven's drive the following morning. The lights were lit at the front of the house, however, and Miles saw a hired coach parked before the front steps.

"A busy morning at the manor," he remarked to Desiree, who was sitting opposite him.

"Miss Pollehn must be leaving," she said. "Yes, there she is, loading her cats into the coach."

"An unusual woman. A pity she must depart in dishonor."

Desiree met his eyes directly. "In her situation it would be difficult not to be unusual, I think. I spoke with her at some length last evening. She's not very attractive, which is a handicap for a woman, as you know; perhaps a worse handicap than for a man to be born without legs."

Surprised, Miles said nothing. As each day passed Desiree seemed more comfortable with him, and her silences were becoming increasingly rare. When she spoke, it was not frivolously, but with the gravity of a grandmother. He still could not get used to it.

Desiree continued. "She's never felt accepted, not even by her friends. She believes they only tolerate her out of Christian duty. Therefore she's become attached to her cats and has always tried to distinguish herself by study. At heart she is a very lonely woman."

"I feel sorry for her then," he said.

"Perhaps there's no need for sorrow any longer," she replied with a slight smile.

"Very mysterious." He tilted his head. "You may be sixteen on the outside, but I suspect that whatever lies within you is much older than I."

Her smile widened. "Perhaps."

He contemplated her, thinking how much she resembled his mother in good intentions, though he had not observed her long enough to know if she was capable of half the good deeds. Still, she appeared to exemplify everything that was deified in womanhood: a quiet spirit, an understanding heart, a love for children, a desire to help. He had always teased Roslyn about wanting her to act in a similar manner. Now that he was betrothed to a stunning young woman who possessed the very qualities he admired most, he could only think: *What a fine sister she would make.*

Only God knew how he was going to be able to marry her.

As the viscount's coach pulled to a stop, Roslyn and her father emerged from the house. Seconds later, Jonathan rounded the corner of the manor leading his horse. Roger Crim trailed behind, his feet scuffing the gravel as though every step grew heavier.

After greeting Desiree and Miles, Roslyn moved to Harriet's hired coach to make her good-byes, or so he supposed. *Wonder if I should say anything, or leave well—or poor —alone.*

He was destined to be spared the decision.

"Pardon me, pardon me," Roger Crim said, pushing through the travelers to Miss Pollehn's coach with the air of one who has come to a sudden decision and must hasten before changing his mind. "Oh, beg pardon for a minute, Miss Roslyn, please. There's a thing I need to say to Miss Pollehn."

Roslyn moved aside, her expression so bemused that Miles fought a smile. It was unlike the groom to act so assertive.

Hurrying, the viscount tossed Roslyn's valise to his driver and spoke quietly with Mr. Andrews while he waited for Roslyn to have her moment with Harriet. During that interval, Victoria joined them looking charmingly sleepy in an unpressed muslin gown and with her hair flowing over her shoulders.

Miles was conscious of Jonathan edging closer, anxious to be on the move. He was not alone in that. The viscount sent Roslyn a look begging for haste. It was then that Miss Pollehn screamed, threw open the door of her coach, and jumped to the ground, practically throwing Roger over.

"Mr. Crim is returning with me!" she shouted. "He's going to work for my family while we become better acquainted!"

"Here, what's this?" bellowed Mr. Andrews.

Roger pulled off his hat and turned the brim

round and round in his hands. "I'll be leaving you, sir, but you don't need a groom anyway. Not without a stable. And as Lord Beaumont is putting up most of the animals for you, you can do with just a stable boy for a time. I want to thank you for keeping me on all these years, but . . ." He blushed furiously. "It's time to follow my heart, just like Miss Highton said to me last night."

The viscount's incredulous eyes moved to Desiree, who had remained in his coach but seemed to be enjoying the drama from its open window.

"Miss Highton?" repeated Mr. Andrews, looking like murder.

"Before I joined you last night at dinner," she explained, "I visited Miss Pollehn and then spoke with Mr. Crim for a few moments. I made no suggestions, only listened. Mr. Crim's decision is entirely his own."

"And I'll be forever grateful for your listening ears," Roger said. "She helped me understand that Miss Pollehn was so smart she might overlook it that I'm beneath her, and she was right! Miss Highton, I'll be in your debt evermore."

"We both will," Harriet gushed. "Oh, isn't it wonderful? Only imagine if Roger hadn't said anything; I'd never have known he had tender feelings for me." She took his hand. "Such a silly man to think I'd be bothered by his station in life. We're all who we are because of the accident of birth, aren't we? And Roger has had little opportunity for improvement, but now he will, under my glad tutelage! Oh, it is so—"

"All right, all right!" growled Mr. Andrews. "Be

off with the both of you before you turn my stomach!"

Harriet spun gaily to her coach, flung the door open wide again, and paused to wave. As she did, her three cats raced out, one fleeing in the direction of the woods, the other two heading directly for the party standing in the drive. Miles moved instinctively to the side; unfortunately, Mr. Andrews chose the same direction. A streak of yellow wound around the older man's ankle, then howled and swerved to bite when he accidentally stepped on its tail.

Thurmond fell backward, his leg twisting beneath him.

Miles could not determine who shrieked, whether Roslyn or Victoria. Perhaps both. They stooped to Andrews's side at the same time, both exclaiming in frightened voices, their words a muddle beneath Thurmond's shouts.

"Bring my pistol! Someone bring my pistol and I'll make an end of these animals from Hell, I swear!"

"You cannot mean it!" Harriet cried. "Oh, Roger, hurry and catch them! We must find my babies!"

Victoria said, "I'm so sorry, Mr. Andrews! You must be in terrible pain, but you're being very brave."

"Father, how is your leg?" Roslyn said. "Can you walk?"

"Walk? I can't even get up with the two of you hovering over me like I was dying. Miles, here! Help me rise!"

The viscount had already extended his hand, but when the older gentleman rose to his feet, his face went white. Quickly, Miles steadied him, and Jonathan moved to the victim's other side. They moved him inside and to a chair in the parlor.

After a quick examination, the viscount found no broken bones, though the gentleman's ankle had swollen so badly that Marsden was called to fetch scissors to cut off the boot. When Roslyn demanded that a physician be sent for to tend his bruises, Jonathan stepped forward and reminded her of the need for haste. Miles admired his restraint; he had been expecting him to explode at any moment.

Roslyn said, "Perhaps I shouldn't go . . ."

"Well, don't stay on my account," Thurmond said irritably. "The wound isn't mortal."

She hesitated. "Are you certain you don't need me?"

"He'll be fine, Roslyn," Victoria said earnestly. "I'll make sure he's cared for properly, never fear."

"There, you see?" Thurmond said.

Roslyn scowled. Miles saw her waver, then slowly look to him. For her own safety, he knew she should stay. Yet he found himself seizing her hand. "Come. You won't rest if we leave you behind."

Nodding, Roslyn kissed Andrews's forehead and exited the house.

* * *

Once under way, the foursome within the coach quickly fell into a groggy silence. Miles leaned into the corner and was soon dreaming, waking only when Desiree's head lolled against his shoulder. She looked even more like an angelic child in sleep, and he was surprised when protective feelings stirred. He sat up, taking care not to awaken her. Across from him, Roslyn watched Desiree, then met his eyes with a sad little smile. Jonathan took no notice of anyone, his gaze set on the passing scenery.

Near midmorning, the viscount's driver stopped the coach at an inn to rest the horses. The travelers moved inside to the tavern, a medium-sized room with limestone walls darkened with soot. An unlit fireplace gaped along one wall, its hearth littered with ashes. Two leaded windows admitted meager light. There was a candle at each table, however, and a few of them flickered weakly, illuminating the scattered customers in the room.

"Bread and cheese," Jonathan said when the host came to their table. "As fast as you can."

"And fresh fruit if you have it," Roslyn said. Meeting Jonathan's stare, she said defensively, "I don't mean to eat it here. We can carry the food with us in the carriage."

Miles calmly requested a joint of beef, then said, "The horses need a decent interval. Ten more minutes won't matter."

"How can you be certain?" The lines at the side of Jonathan's mouth deepened. "Every second we delay could prove more disastrous for Miss Cummings."

"Do you think I don't know it?" Roslyn cried. "You're not the only one concerned about her, Jonathan. She's been my friend for years and is extremely dear to me."

He lowered his eyes. "My pardon." An uneasy quiet fell until the innkeeper appeared with ale for the gentlemen and tea for the ladies. When he left, Jonathan added, "It's only that . . . if I were on horseback, I'd be able to travel twice as fast."

Roslyn's eyes flashed. "Of course you could, but have you considered that you need us with you for Esther's peace of mind? It's possible, is it not, that she might view a rescue by a solitary gentleman, no matter how well intended, as another abduction?"

Jonathan flushed and fell silent.

Desiree said, "I think she would trust Mr. Leffew, but she *will* be more comfortable among other women. Sometimes gentlemen can be so commanding that a lady can't think clearly. Men always believe they know best, isn't that true? I suppose because you're so physically strong. But strength doesn't necessarily mean wisdom. Women are capable of thinking for themselves if given the chance."

With rounded eyes, Roslyn lifted her cup in a salute. "I have often said the same."

"Yes, you have," Miles said. "I hope you're not letting her influence you, Miss Highton."

Desiree smiled. "It's only what I've observed."

She sipped her tea. "There is a thing that worries me, though. All of you seem to expect Miss Cummings will return with you. I hope you won't be too disappointed if she puts the needs of her family above her own. She might view our offer for freedom as an unthinkable road to follow."

Miles had considered that possibility to be quite likely, but he said nothing. The darkness that fell across Jonathan's face forestalled further conversation on the matter.

Later, while the ladies refreshed themselves upstairs, Miles and Jonathan walked outside. The day was fine, with an almost cloudless sky and a slight breeze. Charles, the viscount's driver, had pulled the carriage closer to the inn and was ready to leave.

And so was Jonathan, if the furrows in his brow were any indication. His impatience had burdened Miles all morning. With each mile that passed, the viscount became more convinced he'd been right to worry about the gentleman's emotional state.

"Your concern for Miss Cummings does you credit," Miles said carefully.

The look Jonathan turned upon him could have sliced ice. "Only a brick wall would fail to be concerned for her."

"Yes, but you seem especially touched by her situation."

"She's a brave young woman without a defender. Think of the courage it took to disguise herself as a boy to escape for a mere fortnight, and now she's not even to be allowed that. And in spite of her . . . hardships, she has only the best to say for everyone. To possess such kindness, such grace . . . such sweetness . . ." Words failing him, he shook his head.

He's a thousand fathoms deep, Miles thought, his heart drumming with anxiety. "I'm glad you value those traits, since your betrothed exhibits every one of them."

The clouds in Jonathan's eyes suddenly cleared. "Yes, of course. Well, Roslyn hasn't had the problems that Miss Cummings has endured, and . . ."

"And what?" Miles growled.

Jonathan's gaze skittered away from the viscount's. He removed his hat. Ran his fingers through his hair. Put the hat back on. "During the past week, I've been in her presence for greater lengths of time than ever before. And . . ."

"And?" the viscount prompted dangerously.

"Well . . . sometimes she is a bit . . . outspoken, have you noticed?"

"No," Miles lied, his anxiety warming to anger.

"I'm surprised if you haven't; you've known her longer than I. And occasionally her responses lack a certain . . . gentleness . . . even femininity."

"Is that what you think? For myself, I've never met a more feminine and gentle woman. Perhaps she doesn't display it in all the typical ways, but that only makes her more intriguing. I thank God that she's not one of those fawning women who only opens her mouth to speak when she's certain she won't contradict my opinion. How tedious that would be."

Leffew stared. Something flickered behind his eyes. "I'm not disparaging her," he said in softer tones. "Roslyn is desirable in every way. I consider myself . . . fortunate . . . to be her future husband."

"You should." The viscount stepped closer. "Try to remember that, will you?"

Roslyn and Desiree emerged from the inn. Miles walked stiffly forward, offered them both an arm, and assisted the ladies into the carriage. He was conscious of Leffew watching him the entire time.

Let him wonder, Miles thought. *A little competition might stir the cobwebs from his brain, make him see the worth of the prize he's won.* If Leffew thought he could trod on Roslyn's feelings and get away with it, he was due for a surprise.

Fifteen

They arrived in Essex before six and in the hamlet of Daiden shortly afterward. Deeply forested and with a tributary dividing the village's quaint shops, an arched wooden bridge uniting the halves, the place was picturesque, Miles supposed. Or it would have been had anyone the calmness of mind to appreciate it.

Perhaps Desiree did. She gazed through the window with a pleasant look on her face, strange child. But then, she was less entangled with the principals involved.

Charles slowed the carriage in front of a bakery and asked an old man sweeping the sidewalk for directions. Within moments they were out of town again and turning down a narrow lane to wind through acres of heavy woods. A lonely place ripe for ghostly tales, Miles thought.

The road seemed to go on for miles, but after the lane took a final, wooded turn to the right, Esther's home was revealed at last. While large, the residence appeared to be little more than a glorified farmhouse. Years had passed since it had last been painted, and the timbers along the roofline were beginning to rot.

A lad ran eagerly from the stables to tend the horses, but became distracted by the Beaumont crest on the carriage door, exclaiming at its colors and running his finger along its border. Maybe the Cummings family didn't have company often.

As Roslyn and Desiree gathered their reticules, Miles said, "Perhaps it's best if Jonathan and I go first."

"I haven't traveled all this way to be left sitting in a coach like some useless creature," Roslyn said. "If we're to be turned away, I at least want to place my feet on Esther's property."

Jonathan met his eyes with a knowing look, but Miles refused to respond. "You're perfectly right," he said instead, then stepped out of the coach and lifted his hand to assist her. He stifled a laugh when she didn't move right away but sat staring at him as if she could not believe her ears.

There was no need to knock when they arrived at the door; a boy of about ten years flung it open before Miles could lift his hand, and demanded to know who they were. When the viscount told the flaxen-haired child they were looking for Esther Cummings, he closed the door to a crack and yelled for his father.

A minute passed, then two as the sound of running feet and garbled shouts filtered through the door. Roslyn began to bite her lip. Miles squeezed her hand encouragingly.

"Enough of this," Jonathan muttered. "We should force our way inside."

"England is still a civilized country," Miles told him, sympathy gone. He found it difficult to grasp the change in Leffew's personality. Prior to the past week, the man had never said or done anything that went beyond the rules of the strictest propriety.

Did love make everyone insane?

Finally the door swung open to reveal a thin, frail-looking woman wearing a gown twenty years out of date, its floral print faded to a gray monotone. "Yes?" she said tentatively, looking from one face to another with apprehensive eyes.

Jonathan stepped forward, nudging Miles to the side to the viscount's vast irritation. "Is Miss Cummings here?"

"Yes," she answered slowly, her voice high and tense as a violin string, a voice accustomed to whining, Miles sensed immediately. An annoying voice.

"Is she safe?" Jonathan demanded. "Has Ames—is she wed yet?"

The woman's mouth opened and her chin wobbled as she gazed at Leffew. He was frightening her, and no wonder from the fierce look in his eyes. Miles pushed back to the center, regaining his place and preparing to make proper introductions, but then Roslyn took his arm and he looked at her instead.

"Are you Esther's mother? I'm her friend Roslyn Andrews from Montrose Academy."

"Oh well then," the woman said, relief in her tone. "I've heard so much about you, Roslyn. I suppose you can come in, but I hope you're not going to be difficult about my daughter."

They were admitted into a dusty hall, then invited to sit in a small parlor cluttered with aging, mismatched pieces and countless paintings of farm animals on the walls. Roslyn cut Miles a pert look as she passed inside.

The minx, proud she'd shown she wasn't a *useless creature*. A few moments alone and he'd kiss away that smug air of hers. The temptation to allow his imagination to run riot could not be resisted; and when he came to himself, introductions had been made and Mrs. Cummings was fawning over him, a viscount in her home, and wouldn't her mother be impressed if she were alive?

"But what about your daughter?" Jonathan pressed.

"What *about* my daughter?" said a voice from the hall. A man of middle years entered, looking almost as fragile as his wife. Short of stature with gaunt wrists showing beyond his cuffs, Mr. Cummings did not present the dreadful image Miles had been expecting. He looked exceptionally meek, in fact, with his bland, round face; spectacles; and—but for a fringe of hair circling in back—bald head.

Jonathan stood with effort, the springs in the sofa being so near the floor. "Is she married?"

"Her marriage has been arranged for next Saturday," Cummings said. "I suppose you've come to see her, but I'm sorry to say she can't take visitors."

"Why not?" Jonathan shot back. "Is she injured?"

The older man blinked at him. "No. She's confined to her room for running away from home."

"Don't think us cruel for punishing her," Mrs. Cummings said to Miles, her high-pitched drone making his hackles rise. "She terrified us. Can you imagine how I felt when she ran off? What an awful thing to do to one's mother! I never would have, I can tell you that. *My* mother would've locked me in the attic for years."

"She was worried about her marriage," Roslyn said. "She didn't know what else to do."

"We know all that." Cummings sat on the edge of a threadbare chair. "Young girls often get missish before their wedding."

"Missish?" Roslyn glared at him. "Are you aware that she's betrothed to a dangerous man? I've seen the bruises on her arms."

"Bruises!" Jonathan's fingers knotted into fists.

Mr. Cummings gave him a startled look over the top of his spectacles. "Braxton isn't dangerous, just impulsive. He'll calm down after they're wed."

"He's a fine young man," Mrs. Cummings told Miles. "Our Esther is fortunate he chose her, what with his wealth and handsome looks. All the girls in the village chased after him, but it was our daughter who caught his eye. It's a good thing she took after my side of the family."

Fortunately there was no need to respond to this, as Miles and the others were distracted by the entry of six boys varying in age between five

and seventeen from the look of them—all of them
blonde, although the hair of the two taller ones
had darkened to ash. They took positions wher-
ever they found a space, some dropping to the
floor, one even perching on the arm of the viscount's chair.

Miles felt caged in by the lads' curious eyes and
youthful energy, especially as there could be no
question days had passed since their last baths.
He could not understand why they were being allowed to crowd into a room designed to seat four
adults comfortably.

"My sons," Cummings said proudly, and began
naming them. The viscount caught a William and
a Ted, but after that his mind balked. "Esther's
marriage will make it possible for them to attend
the finest schools, something I haven't been able
to provide since our steward—well, no need to go
into that or I shall make myself livid. Esther's was
the only proper education I could manage."

"Money well spent, too," said Mrs. Cummings.
"Her being gone awhile made Mr. Ames's heart
grow fonder."

"I had hoped it would make him forget me,"
Esther said breathlessly from the doorway.
"Jonathan, you *are* here; I thought I heard your
voice. I'm so glad you've recovered. I was out of
my mind with worry—oh, and Roslyn! Lord Beaumont, er, Miles. And Miss—"

"Esther Catherine Cummings!" cried her
mother.

"How did you get out?" exclaimed her father.

"I have always known how, Papa," she said,

stepping into the room. "I can pick the lock with my hairpin. Oh, it's so good to see all of you! But why are you here?"

"We were worried about you," Jonathan said, the muscles in his face going soft as melting butter.

"Oh, but you shouldn't have worried," Esther said, her glowing expression contradicting her words. "That is, I know Braxton and I left rather unconventionally—his striking you was unforgivable, and please understand that I wouldn't leave your side until I was certain you were breathing. And then, when he refused to allow me to say anything when we arrived back at Misthaven, I was beside myself, although I had the hope that Roslyn and the others would find you on their way home. I have done nothing except pray for your recovery since."

She pulled a handkerchief from her sleeve and dabbed at her eyes, smiling bravely. "But I did leave word for Roslyn that I would be all right. Truly, you shouldn't have troubled yourselves to follow me all this way."

Esther's speech, Miles noted, was directed exclusively to Jonathan, her cheeks rosy with excitement. The gown she wore, though a simple morning dress with mint-green checks, was of much finer material and workmanship than that of her family's. Gilding the lily, he thought cynically. The parents devoting all their funds to their one hope, a beautiful and charming daughter. What a gamble. No wonder they had closed their eyes to Ames's flaws.

"I . . . none of us could rest without knowing your fate," Jonathan said simply, moving a pace nearer. "Are you well? He didn't harm you?"

Out of the dozen and more people in the parlor, they were the only two standing. Miles suddenly felt himself at a play watching a tragedy about doomed lovers.

His gaze flew to Roslyn. He prayed she wouldn't sense the attraction between them and become hurt. But she did see it; her eyes were misty as she observed them. In truth, only an unfeeling piece of wood could fail to note how Jonathan and Esther saw only each other. Still, he blamed himself for planting the suggestion in her mind.

Unable to view her wretchedness any longer, he lowered his gaze to the floor.

"There's no need to worry," Esther said softly. "I'm fine."

"Thank God for that. But you won't be fine a week from now when you marry the arsonist."

Esther's eyes grew round. "Arsonist?"

Roslyn explained, "Mr. Ames set a fire in our stable to divert us from following you immediately. It burned to the ground."

"Oh, Papa," Esther moaned, one hand flying to her heart. "Do you understand now how troubled he is?"

"You must be mistaken," said her father, pushing his spectacles higher on his nose. "Braxton wouldn't do that."

"Our groom saw him setting the fire," Roslyn said.

"That's impossible!" Mrs. Cummings shrilled.

"No doubt your groom did it, then blamed his deed on Braxton."

Mr. Cummings nodded. "Yes, that makes far more sense."

They wouldn't believe wrong of Ames if he murdered Esther in front of them, Miles saw. The young woman's tears were flowing again, and in another minute Leffew would have her in his arms.

The viscount slid forward, dislodging the boy on his chair and apologizing, but he needed a clearer view of Roslyn should she need his support. God bless her, there was a strange expression on her face, like someone experiencing a sudden realization. The only other time he could recall her looking like that was when she offered him her last piece of bread the afternoon they were lost in a cave.

That had been the day of their first kiss, he recalled fondly.

"Come back with us," Jonathan was saying.

Esther, her eyes shining, regarded him speechlessly.

"Roslyn and I want to offer you the permanent hospitality of our home," he continued.

Mr. Cummings leaped to his feet. "What you are suggesting is unthinkable! Esther cannot break her engagement and live off charity!"

"What will become of her brothers if she acts so selfishly?" cried his wife.

"I can help them," Jonathan said. "And you as well. I have sufficient."

Esther held up a restraining hand. "No. No,

thank you, Jonathan . . . Roslyn. But you do see it's impossible."

"No, it isn't."

Roslyn spoke with such conviction that, even had she not walked to stand between Esther and Jonathan, every eye would have centered on her.

Esther briefly pressed Roslyn's arm. "Thank you, my dear, but it's simply not feasible."

"And why not?" Roslyn said. "You love him, don't you?"

The viscount stumbled to his feet.

Esther's hands flew to her cheeks, her startled gaze seeking Jonathan's, then dropping in shame.

Leffew snapped, "Roslyn, how could you speak to her so?"

Roslyn gave him a soft, knowing look. "And *you* love *her.*" When he reddened and began to shake his head, she said, "You don't deny it, do you?"

There was a long silence during which no one breathed. When Miles thought he couldn't bear another instant of watching Roslyn's trembling lips, Jonathan finally spoke.

"No. Forgive me, Roslyn, but I would be lying if I said I don't love her." Esther burst into tears. Jonathan leaned toward her, then pulled back with a regretful look at his betrothed. "Of course, I'm very fond of you as well and will be a faithful husband as I've promised."

"You cad," Miles said between his teeth. "Will you also feed her crumbs beneath the table?"

"Thank you, Miles," Roslyn said, "but don't be angry for what can't be helped. Fond is not enough for me, Jonathan. I release you."

Leffew stared, too stunned to speak.

"Our engagement is broken." Roslyn removed her sapphire ring and dropped it into Jonathan's hand. Then she lifted one of Esther's hands and placed it in Jonathan's. "The rest I leave to you."

"Roslyn, I . . . I don't know what to say." Leffew's face looked lit within as he returned his attention to Esther.

Silently, her eyes lowering, Roslyn reclaimed her seat. She did not look up. Her fingers locked together on her lap.

Miles was shattered and so proud of Roslyn he could hardly draw breath. *What must that effort have cost her?* He moved to her chair and stood beside it, placing a supportive hand on her shoulder.

"Oh, Roslyn," Esther suddenly cried. "There has been nothing between us, I promise you! I would never betray our friendship, even though I have found Jonathan to be quite the best man I've ever known, a man of gentle strength—"

"Enough!" shouted Mr. Cummings. "Esther, you're already engaged, I beg you to remember!"

Jonathan turned on him. "I stand before you ready to ask for your daughter's hand. Are you so unfeeling that you could still expect her to marry a criminal . . . sir?"

"You have no proof of that," Mrs. Cummings said musingly, her gaze assessing Jonathan.

"Merely an eyewitness account of arson," Miles reminded.

Desiree spoke for the first time since entering the room. "If you are concerned for your chil-

220 *Marcy Stewart*

dren's welfare, I believe you need have no fear. Mr. Leffew will be able to provide for them."

"He owns the largest estate in Chawton," Roslyn said, a hint of regret in her voice. Miles squeezed her shoulder in sympathy. Mr. Cummings opened his mouth, then closed it. He shot a glance at his wife.

"How large?" she asked.

Moaning, Esther covered her face with her hands. Jonathan smiled, tugged her fingers loose, restored them within his, then began to speak swiftly of acres and properties and pounds. When he finished, Mrs. Cummings's eyes were round as an owl's.

"That's ten thousand more a year than Ames," said her husband in a wondering voice.

"But Braxton will be very angry if she doesn't go through with the wedding," Mrs. Cummings observed.

Her husband nodded. "Esther will be in danger every minute. He'll likely steal her away for a clandestine marriage."

"Or worse!" squealed his wife.

Now they were willing to see Ames's character without blinders, Miles thought, raising one eyebrow.

"Perhaps we shouldn't wait, then," Jonathan said. "Esther and I could go to Gretna Green right away and take the wind from his sails."

"Not without me as chaperone," said Mrs Cummings, her gaze piercing Leffew. "You can bring me home after the wedding."

A curtain fell over Jonathan's eyes. "Naturally;

that will be most appropriate." Brightening, he pulled Esther's hands closer to his heart. "If she's willing, that is."

"Nothing would make me happier, except—" She sent a melancholy gaze toward Roslyn. "Perhaps it would be best to wait a decent interval; it might not be easy to explain, our sudden marriage—"

"Don't worry about me," Roslyn said, and Miles's spirit lifted to see the starch return to her eyes. "I'll blame everything on Jonathan. By the time you return from your wedding trip, all Chawton will be at my feet."

"As they should," Jonathan said, and with trembling hands placed the sapphire on Esther's finger. Smiles and excited chatter broke out all round; even Roslyn watched the radiant couple with happiness, though her eyes were wistful. Miles gazed at her until she returned his look; then he bent to whisper in her ear.

"I've never seen a finer sacrifice. You're the best person I've ever known."

Her lips curved upward. "Excepting your mother, of course."

"Excepting no one." Her cheek lay very closely to his, temptingly close. Such beautiful skin, smooth as a pane of glass but radiating warmth and life. He stroked her face with his eyes, for he dared not touch her as he wished. Lowering his voice further, he drew closer to her ear. "There's much more I'd like to say to you."

"But you cannot," she whispered back. "Oh,

Miles, what am I going to do? Father will slay me for this."

Before he could respond, Mrs. Cummings suddenly shrieked, "Braxton is coming to dinner tonight at eight! We must be packed and away before then!"

Sixteen

"I'm not afraid of Braxton Ames," Jonathan said stoutly. "I welcome the chance to meet him again."

There will be a duel, Roslyn thought. In her anxiety she clutched the hand resting on her shoulder, and felt Miles tighten his fingers around hers.

Esther went pale. "Please, Jonathan, I beg you, let us be gone. He'll be very angry at first, but once he learns I'm married and there's no point in bothering with me, he'll recover. There's no need for unpleasantness."

"Night will be falling soon." Jonathan's husky tones and sibilant pronunciations gave Roslyn a *frisson* of foreboding; it was unbelievable how dangerous he could sound under the proper conditions. "I have no taste for flying away like a frightened wren, not when I owe him . . . so much."

"If you won't hurry for yourself, mayhaps you will on my behalf." Esther folded her hands and brought them below her chin in a supplicating manner. "Have you thought what might happen to *me* if something should happen to *you*?"

Jonathan could not deny her, not when her eyes gazed into his with such longing and fear. He acquiesced in a soft, crooning voice that startled Roslyn almost as much as his threatening one had. He must be in love; he'd certainly never spoken to her like that. Had he done so, she wouldn't have been able to help herself; she would have laughed.

The house immediately flew into an uproar. The oldest son was dispatched with Miles to rent a carriage in the village. Mr. Cummings began to lead Jonathan through the house and point out repairs that needed to be made. Mrs. Cummings squawked orders and flew back and forth between Esther's room and her own, exclaiming she had nothing to wear. Her sons gathered trunks from a storage room on the upper floor, the sounds of their stomping feet like thunder overhead.

"That was a brave gesture you made," Desiree said to Roslyn when they were left alone in the parlor. "I hope your feelings for Mr. Leffew didn't run too deep."

The girl's voice held just the right note of empathy, and Roslyn saw no reason to be silent. "I'm very fond of Jonathan, but my father desired the match more than I."

"Fathers can be very demanding, can't they? Mine was, although he always believed he had my best interests at heart."

"And didn't he?" Roslyn's pulse began to race. Was it possible that Desiree was unhappy in her betrothal and would now, stimulated by the past moments, declare her desire to be free of Miles?

Did such things happen in real life or only in fairy tales? She sent a quick prayer heavenward.

"In his mind he did. Of course, in regard to Lord Beaumont, I couldn't be more pleased with Papa's selection. I'd never be able to find a finer husband on my own." She chuckled. "When we came to Oakwood, I was very nervous thinking the viscount would be proud and haughty. Instead I've been pleasantly surprised at his character. And naturally he is very handsome."

"Mmm," Roslyn murmured wretchedly.

"And his mother will make an outstanding mother-in-law."

"Oh, yes." Roslyn jumped to her feet, crossed her arms tightly over her middle, and went to stare out the window.

Within the hour the household and visitors gathered in the front garden to make their good-byes beside the battered green coach Miles had hired in the village. With Jonathan at her side, Esther embraced each brother in turn, then her father. Finally arriving at Roslyn, she gave her a prolonged, tearful hug.

"I'll never be able to thank you enough," Esther choked out weepily. "In giving up Jonathan, you've done more for me than anyone ever has. You've saved my life."

"I'm glad you're happy," Roslyn said, meaning it even though envy flared in her heart. Would she ever smile as Esther was, joy beaming from every pore? Were it not for her slippers anchoring her to earth, she looked ready to float into the clouds.

But such airiness didn't lie in *Roslyn's* future. Desiree *couldn't be more pleased with Papa's selection.* And Miles was not the kind of man who broke promises, especially not one he'd made to his late father.

She suddenly realized Esther was still talking, and was ashamed to wish her gone.

"Who would ever have thought love could come so quickly?" Esther was saying. "Remember when we giggled about the possibility at Montrose? I never thought love at first sight could be real until I met Jonathan. Somehow I knew we were destined for one another from our earliest moments. Yet we couldn't have acted upon it were it not for your unselfishness."

"I'm not so unselfish," Roslyn said uncomfortably.

"Yes, you are. Oh, and only think. I'll be living so near Misthaven that we'll be able to visit every week! And someday love will come again for you. I know it. If necessary, I'll help you find that special person. Jonathan must have many friends; I could plan a dinner; no, a house party would be even better. Then you could stay with us, and—"

"Esther," Roslyn said hastily, "your mother is sending you a look."

"She always is," Esther said, glancing over her shoulder. "For myself," she added *sotto voce*, "I believe you and Lord Beaumont would make a handsome couple, though I suppose since you've grown up together you think of each other as siblings."

Roslyn, reminding herself that her friend knew

nothing of Miles's engagement, managed to force a laugh and shake her head. Fortunately, at that moment Mrs. Cummings, who was being assisted into the coach by her husband, shouted for them to hurry; and after a final flurry of farewells, they were off.

When the coach disappeared around the bend, silence descended over the group left behind. Miles was regarding her with compassion, and his sympathy made her feel even lower. She shrugged her shoulders and suggested they leave as well.

"You could stay the night," Mr. Cummings rushed to say. "My wife left a threesome of ducks roasting on the spit for supper. There's some potatoes and such, too."

"Worried about Ames, are you?" Miles asked in a dry voice.

"Yes," he admitted, his gaze assessing the viscount head to foot. "I'm no match for him, but you are."

With a regretful look at Roslyn, Miles said, "We'll stay."

The dining chamber was a smallish room on the opposite side of the hall, and Roslyn could see its well-scarred table from her seat in the parlor. The single servant of the house, a maid who looked no older than thirteen, had just begun to set the table when Braxton Ames arrived.

Mr. Cummings waved Miles over; he didn't want to answer the door alone. Roslyn and Desiree exchanged a worried glance.

Why did Miles have to be so brave? Why did he have to fight Jonathan's battles for him?

As the door swung open, Ames sighted Miles. "So it is you. I saw the carriage and thought it might be. What are you doing here?"

"Just a friendly visit," Miles said.

"No friend of mine."

Mr. Cummings mumbled an invitation to come inside but not to insult his guests. Ames strode past him and into the parlor like a strong wind. Roslyn thought she'd never met anyone with such an aura of energy about him, and all of it hostile so far as she'd seen. Such a shame, too, for he would be quite handsome if not for that spoiled child expression on his face.

He made a grudging greeting to the ladies and nodded at the boys, his eyes moving restlessly. As Miles and Mr. Cummings followed him into the room, he swerved and demanded to know where Esther was.

Roslyn wanted to close her ears to what followed. She did manage to avert her eyes from much of the young man's devastation when he learned of Esther's flight. But caution led her to watch him carefully when, as she expected, his anguish changed to rage.

"You let her do this?" he demanded of Mr. Cummings, who shrank backward with his fingers splayed before him.

"She was very insistent," he said. "Couldn't say no to her."

"Liar. You've been denying her for years. You can't dismiss one engagement for another; that isn't civilized. Out of my way, both of you! I'm going after her."

"No," Miles said in mild tones, "you're not."

When Ames smiled, Roslyn felt a crackle of danger lash toward the viscount. Immediately she stood. In an instant he eyed her dismissively, as a serpent would measure a mouse.

"And who will stop me?" He very nearly made a melody of the words. *"Her?"*

"No, I will." The viscount moved a menacing pace closer to him.

"Step outside and we shall see."

"I don't feel inclined to fisticuffs, thank you."

Roslyn felt his words like a blow to the stomach. What was wrong with her, feeling so disappointed? She didn't want Miles to get hurt.

"Hah! Just as I expected from a lily-livered *peer!*"

"Lily-livered?" murmured Miles, sounding bored. "You're as original as slop in a pig trough. Actually, I was rather thinking of reporting your criminal acts to the local magistrate. We have witnessed accounts of your assault on Jonathan Leffew and your act of arson—enough to lock you away for a while if not hang you."

Ames gazed at him with wild eyes. He was panting like a wild beast. A long interval passed during which Roslyn convinced herself that Miles had not acted cowardly and had been right not to resort to violence; threats were a much more humane way to deal with someone of Ames's lability.

Just as she was beginning to relax, Ames sprang catlike across the room and seized her in front of him with one arm at her waist, the other at her throat. She pulled against the one at her neck, but his arms were iron and before she could blink he'd pulled both her hands to the small of her back. Immediately her head lolled backward; she could not breathe, he was pressing against her neck, he was choking her, her fingers weren't free or she'd claw at his eyes, she could hear Desiree screaming.

"I have a better idea," Ames said loudly. "This woman—Miss Andrews, is it?—and I will search for Esther. When we find her, Esther and I will go on to Gretna Green, and Miss Andrews can do as she pleases. In the meantime, you won't follow us or I'll snap her head like a twig, do you understand?"

Tell him yes, Roslyn wanted to cry, but she could not even groan. Behind a curtain of tears she saw Miles watching, aghast, as Ames led her past and into the hall.

She visualized the horror awaiting her, an endless ride with *him* holding her and making threats, and at the end, Esther being taken. And where was Miles? Why wouldn't he do anything? Well, of course, he was afraid she'd be hurt, so she'd simply have to help him. Even though no true lady would ever think what she was thinking, she had lived around stallions long enough to know certain things.

She went very limp. As Ames fought to counteract the dead weight, he leaned over, and she kicked upward and back, hard. With an *oomph* of air, he fell to his knees.

The next few moments passed to her complete satisfaction. Ames was not so injured that he couldn't return the viscount's blows, but altogether it wasn't too violent a fight. Several chairs were knocked over, and the Cummings boys had time to circle and cheer before the villain fell into a defeated heap. Miles and the two older children bundled Braxton down to the cellar and locked him in.

"Does that idiot have a surviving parent?" Miles called upward as he mounted the cellar steps. They had all crowded into the hallway to watch the incarceration.

"Both mother and father," Mr. Cummings said.

"Good. He'll keep until tomorrow, then. When we leave, we'll take him to his home. Surely his father will hold him there until he regains his senses, especially after he learns what mischief his son has been playing at. By then Esther will be married."

He had arrived at the top of the stairs, his eyes searching for Roslyn. To her delight, he wrapped his arms around her. "You're trembling," he said softly. "Are you all right?"

"I think so," she said, voice wobbling. She felt weaker at this moment than she had during her entire ordeal. When his beautiful long fingers began to explore the neckline of her gown, probing for damage, she felt the world spin.

"You may have a bruise or two," he said, "but I believe you'll be fine."

"I don't know," she whispered, her knees turning to water. She was aware that people surrounded them, and worst of all, Desiree, but she didn't care. "Perhaps I won't."

He gave her a slow smile. "Don't go faint on me now, Lady Foot. Did they teach you that move at the Academy?"

"You were both very heroic!" Desiree said, her eyes shining. "I have never seen the like." As if cued, Miles released Roslyn, who swayed with the sudden abandonment. "And Lord Beaumont, you're very fast on your feet. I could scarcely see your blows, they were falling so fast. Mr. Ames didn't have a chance against you."

"Well," Miles said. He looked so irresistibly sweet and modest, even with the red spot on his cheek that would doubtless darken by tomorrow, that Roslyn bit her tongue to keep from forcing his arms back around her.

Desiree's eyes skimmed the interested faces in the corridor, her expression lively with the need for discretion, yet eager to say more. When she spoke, the words fairly burst from her.

"What a wonderful husband and father you will make! So protective, so very brave!"

Seventeen

When the travelers arrived back at Misthaven on the following evening, Desiree claimed to be very tired; therefore Miles stayed only long enough to unload Roslyn's valise before driving away with his betrothed. Roslyn gazed after them from the doorway of her home until the carriage rolled out of sight, then slipped indoors with a sigh.

The house was strangely quiet as she passed over the threshold. Questioning Marsden, she was told that Miss Sheridan and some of the others were on the terrace; he'd last seen Mr. Andrews in the library.

"You were unable to rescue Miss Cummings?" he asked.

His normally aloof eyes had thawed to something approaching concern, so Roslyn said, "She's fine. I'll explain later, but first I must find Father." Thinking of the interview ahead, she couldn't suppress a chill. In the interest of delay, she asked, "Did Harriet finally depart with Roger yesterday?"

Marsden's expression grew chilly. "Yes, but with

only one cat. The others are in the woods and will soon multiply to thousands, I have no doubt."

"That's good," Roslyn murmured, her head throbbing with possible excuses for breaking off with Jonathan. Perhaps she could claim it was *his* idea . . . but no, liars were always found out. Lifting her chin, she glided down the corridor as a queen might approach the guillotine.

When she arrived at the door to the library, she stared mindlessly at the circle of twining leaves carved at its center. *I am not really here. I'll explain everything to my father as one would tell a story: detached and impersonally. When he explodes, I shall simply go to my room and stay there until he recovers his temper.*

She knocked boldly and threw open the door. Her father sat enthroned in his favorite chair with his injured foot resting on the ottoman, a fire crackling cozily in the hearth. Victoria was sitting in his lap, her arm draped around his shoulders as she kissed him. At Roslyn's entrance, both looked up with startled eyes.

Roslyn screamed and bolted from the room.

"Wait, wait!" Mr. Andrews called after her. "Let me explain!" There was a sound of his cane falling. "Thunderation, but I can't move worth a one-legged dog!"

It was Victoria who caught up with her at the foot of the stairs and with much tearful pleading persuaded her to return to the library. Had Roslyn not been so tired, she was sure she wouldn't have given in so quickly, for the truth was she had no interest in what her father or her former friend had to say. There could be no excuse for such reprehensible behavior, and come tomorrow she would pack her bags and leave. It mattered not that she had no funds; she would find employment as a governess or a maid if necessary—anything to get away from this horrible place she had once called home.

While Roslyn was making her plans, Victoria led her back to the library and closed the door. Now she was trying to direct her onto the settle opposite Mr. Andrews's chair, but Roslyn glared at the fingers on her arm until Victoria released her. Defiantly she sat on the hearth, though it was so low her knees folded to almost the height of her nose, and gazed at her father through narrowed eyes.

"I have asked Victoria to marry me," he said bluntly.

"What?" Roslyn flew to her feet, her head taking a glancing blow from the mantel. Hand flying to the back of her scalp, she said louder, "What did you say?"

Mr. Andrews's voice also rose. "Just now I've asked Victoria to marry me, and she's said yes. I consider myself the most fortunate of men."

I consider you an old fool! Roslyn wanted to shout, but even in her distress she knew better. Instead she said, "I must be asleep in my bed having a hideous nightmare. I cannot have just heard my father say he's betraying the memory of my mother by marrying a woman half his age!"

"Not quite so bad as that," Thurmond said in

hurt tones. "You've always thought me as old as Methuselah, but I'm just forty."

"And I am a little older than you, remember?" Victoria said to Roslyn.

"Yes, two years." Roslyn's mouth twisted with derision. "That makes all the difference, of course.

"Roslyn, I've been alone for over a decade. Your mother would have wanted me to marry again. I know it."

"She wouldn't have wanted you to marry a child!"

Thurmond pounded his cane against the floor. "Enough about age! You and Jonathan aren't quite in the same camp, either, you know!"

"Well, that's neither here nor there, for Jonathan and I are not going to be married!" she burst out.

A taut silence stretched between father and daughter.

"You're not?" Thurmond said finally.

"No, and I won't thank you for shouting at me about it." Too filled with righteous indignation to be fearful now, Roslyn sketched in the happenings of the past thirty-six hours, leaving out nothing. "By now, he and Esther are married," she concluded.

"Well, well," Thurmond said meditatively. "Well."

"I'm so glad," Victoria said with a sigh. "She confided in me this week about her feelings toward him, but begged me not to say anything to you, Roslyn. You were good to give him up."

The last thing she wanted was praise from this buxom viper she'd once loved like a sister. And now she was expected to accept her as a mother? Never in her life.

"And you needn't rail at me about it, Father," Roslyn went on, wondering for an instant why he hadn't already begun to shout protests. "Of course your plans for the estate will go to nothing now, as we won't have any money and must live within our means. I'm sorry the ball was so expensive—" in truth, she wasn't a bit sorry—"and that you won't be able to recoup the loss from Jonathan's pockets after all. Victoria, if you thought by marrying my father you'd achieve wealth and independence, you were sadly mistaken. I'm sure he'll understand if you reconsider your decision."

Victoria regarded her sadly from the settle. "Roslyn, nothing will make me give him up. I've been in love with your father since I was seventeen."

Roslyn started to laugh, then saw how serious Victoria looked. "Surely you jest."

"You don't know, do you?" Victoria's gaze drifted to Thurmond. "You can't see how handsome and commanding your father is and how he could turn a young girl's head."

Roslyn shot a look at her father, who was preening under this accolade, of course. She saw a man of medium height who was not yet too thick in the waist; his hair was dense and brown, his face pleasant, she supposed. She could see nothing remarkable . . . only her father.

"From that Christmas when I entered your house for the first time," Victoria continued, "I knew I'd never met—or ever would meet—anyone like him. I understood my love was hopeless; he was seeing a woman named . . . Miss Malarkey or something like—"

"Miss Muldoon," supplied Roslyn, mesmerized, fumbling blindly behind her to find a chair.

"And each time I drew courage to speak of him afterward, you told me of someone different he was seeing. I knew he viewed me only as a little girl and consigned myself to living my days alone.

"I have had other opportunities, Roslyn. Three gentlemen have asked for my hand; three much younger gentlemen. But I knew I could never give them my heart." Her nose wrinkled in recollection. "I must admit I was suspicious of them, as suitors began to line up only *after* my grandmother passed last year and left me her fortune. I couldn't help doubting their motivation.

"But not your father's. He asked me to be his bride *before* he knew about my inheritance. While I was tending to his ankle less than an hour ago, he suddenly asked me and has made me the happiest woman on earth."

"And me the happiest man," said Thurmond, his eyes tender. "Then when she told me she wished to use her funds to enhance the estate, I felt as if God was shining his light upon me."

"The first thing we shall do is replace that stable." Victoria turned a warm smile upon Roslyn. "For the rest of my days I'll thank you for inviting me here for your house party."

Roslyn's lips twitched upward, then fell.

"Then it doesn't upset you that I'm not marrying Jonathan," she said to her father.

"Of course not," Thurmond replied. "You're free to do as you wish. You can stay with us until your hair turns gray if you like."

"Oh, indeed," Victoria agreed. "It will be like old times, you and me together. And now we shall have Esther nearby, too!"

"Um," Roslyn murmured, then excused herself to look for Colleen. Surely by now the girl had coerced Ned or Gregory into marriage and would soon settle in Chawton, leaving only one of the five of them to face life alone. Herself.

But Colleen had not achieved an engagement, and by the end of the week the girl's loud giggles had all but disappeared. She looked cheered when Gregory promised to write, however, as he stood beside Roslyn and her father before her coach. When the driver cracked his whip, Colleen waved her handkerchief from the window for as long as they could spot her.

Gregory's horse had been brought from Oakwood's stable that morning, and as he swung into the saddle, he thanked them for their hospitality and added, "Colleen is a jolly girl. I shall miss her."

"I think you should marry her," Roslyn said dully.

Gregory threw back his head and laughed. "I'm not quite so impulsive as some. Maybe Ned will

do the honors when he sees how happy Jonathan
and Esther are together." He looked at Roslyn
and winced. "Oh. Sorry."

He waved and set off, the last guest to depart.

The house party had not so much ended as
faded away. Victoria had left two days before to
begin wedding preparations. Ned, having received
a missive from his brother that he and his new
wife would be arriving at the end of the week,
had gone home to make plans for a reception.
And Miles . . . she had not seen Miles since
they'd returned from Essex. He'd sent messages,
quick notes explaining how busy he was and that
Desiree felt unwell, but that was all.

Roslyn moved past her father into the house,
then pulled herself up the stairs to her room. She
was glad to see he was walking without a limp
today, but she didn't want to visit with him. It
wasn't that she was still angry; she would adjust
eventually. No point in feeling sorry for herself.
It was only that she felt too low to speak with *anyone.*

Why hadn't Miles been to see her? She believed
his letters were mere excuses. He didn't *want* to
see her. He was beginning to fall in love with Desiree and couldn't face her.

And not only that; everyone in Chawton felt
sorry for poor Miss Roslyn. As word of Jonathan's
wedding spread, she'd endured a drove of visitors
eager to extend their sympathy . . . and hear
every last detail.

Hetta was changing the linens when Roslyn
reached her room. Suddenly she couldn't abide

her bedchamber or Misthaven a second more. She changed into her riding habit, remembering only when she put on her boots to have Hetta send someone to fetch her horse from Oakwood. What a bother it was, not having a stable.

But when she descended the stairs and left the house fifteen minutes later, she found Miles waiting astride Damon, Northwind's reins looped around his fingers. She breathed in quickly to calm her heart.

"Behold the new stable boy," Miles said.

"You shouldn't have troubled yourself," she said softly.

"But it's been so long since we've ridden together; at least a week. I thought we were overdue."

He has come to tell me he loves Desiree.

After helping her into the saddle, Miles led her in a canter down the drive, then slowed the horses to a walk as they turned onto the lane. He tilted his head and regarded her solemnly.

"You're very quiet," he said.

"Perhaps prolonged separations make me shy."

His chuckle faded away too quickly. "Desiree has been very ill."

"Yes, you said as much in your notes."

"I'm quite worried about her. She's pale and limp as a cloth and can't eat."

Struck with guilt, Roslyn gave him a startled look. "Then she truly *is* ill."

"Yes, haven't I said? The physician is with her at this very moment. I went to fetch him this morning. When I returned to the stable Charlie was saddling Northwind, and I couldn't let the opportunity pass."

"Oh. Perhaps you should be with her now."

"I believe I can be spared a half hour." He peered beneath her hat, searching for her eyes. "All of your guests have gone?"

"Every last one, most either married or engaged."

"A very successful gathering, then." His tone was so cheerful she flinched. "Even though your services weren't necessary for me, you managed to make a great number of matches."

"That's one way of looking at it."

"The rumor I've heard about your father and Miss Pendergrass's betrothal—is it true?"

"Yes." She dared not say more.

"I'm sorry, my dear. I know you feel Victoria will make a dictatorial mistress, but the alliance will be good for your father."

"She'll probably kill him with her—her youthful exuberance."

Miles laughed. "Then at least he'll die happy."

They had reached the top of the lane where the oaks met overhead. Signaling her to follow, the viscount pulled Damon from the road and stopped. When Roslyn drew up beside him with a miserable stare, his eyes filled with so many emotions she could scarce read them all: compassion, pity perhaps; certainly amusement. Before she could take offense, something dark and wild came into his expression and he pulled her toward him in a forceful, all-too-brief kiss.

For a long moment, neither said anything.

When Northwind whinnied and sidled away, Roslyn felt anger rising.

"What can you be thinking, Miles? How can you trifle with me so?"

"I'm not trifling," he said fiercely. "I'm going to marry you."

Her lips parted as hope flared, then died. "You can't."

"But I can, if you'll have me."

"You know I want nothing more, but you're not free." She wanted to weep at his cruelty.

"I'm going to break off the arrangement with Desiree. I don't call it *engagement,* for what my father and hers decided between them isn't honorable enough for that term."

He looked so earnest and intent that her heart thumped faster.

"I've thought deeply about us, Roslyn, about our lives. I've been thinking and debating with myself every day since Ames caught and threatened to harm you. I can't explain what I felt when I saw you in danger. All I can say is that if anything happened to you, my life would be worthless."

"But, Miles, your promise—the estate—"

"I won't deny it pains me to fail my promise, even though my father was wrong in forcing it. But one of the reasons I consented was to protect Mother. And now, because of Desiree's arrival, she knows everything about his behavior and that reason is gone."

He removed his hat and rested it on his thigh, the wind beginning to play with his hair in ways she longed to do. "What honor is there in keeping a promise to the dead if it's done at the expense of the living?"

"But you'll lose Oakwood—"

Miles shook his head, his gaze holding hers. "Oakwood is more than bricks and timber and land. My heritage is in here." He indicated his heart, then his head. "Our children will grow up hearing about it, as will their children. We'll have to live in the city where I can earn our living, but maybe one day we—or one of our descendants— will be able to return to this land and reclaim it."

Even as her heart soared, tears trailed down Roslyn's cheeks. "You'd give up Oakwood . . . for me?"

"It will be less painful than giving *you* up for Oakwood."

His words were the sweetest she'd ever heard; she felt as if she were floating. His decision was impossible, of course, but simply knowing his feelings made all the difference.

"Desiree is ill," she said gently. "You can't hurt her."

"I don't believe her affections are engaged to any degree, but of course I'll wait until she recovers. We'll need to keep this between us only until then."

"Of course," she said dreamily.

"I'm not assuming too much, am I? You're willing to shackle yourself to your old friend who loves you with all he has, pitiful though it may be?"

"My *best* friend. The one I love more than anyone or anything in the world." She couldn't help smiling like a fool as he pulled her toward him for another kiss.

When he was thinking more clearly, he'd reconsider. They wouldn't really be able to be married. His mother would tell him she'd die away from the country. Or Desiree would be found to have a fatal disease, and he would be honor-bound to stand by her. But for the moment she had everything she'd ever hoped for, everything she'd ever needed.

Miles returned to Oakwood a short while later, his heart light, if troubled. He had not spoken impulsively as Roslyn seemed to think; he'd lost sleep every night since their return from Essex, mulling over the implications of his decision. He knew he'd chosen rightly, but that didn't make the future easier.

Trodding through the kitchen to the hall, he lifted the mail from the salver and entered the parlor. His mother was at the secretary adding accounts, and he nodded to her as he thumbed through the missives.

"Has the doctor finished with Desiree?" he asked, sitting on the ottoman, his eyes sharpening on a letter bearing his solicitor's stamp.

"Not yet. Her mother's upstairs, too."

He didn't hear. His attention was too deeply caught by the letter in his hands.

"By all the thunder in heaven," he said a moment later. His mother looked at him in surprise, and he brought the missive to her. "Horace Evans did a small investigation for me. He found out that Desiree Highton is living in a convent in Switzerland."

"What?" cried Lady Beaumont, taking the paper and scanning it rapidly. "I cannot believe it; our guests seem so genuine. Surely there's a mistake."

At that moment, the physician, a short man with a gnarled gray beard, spectacles, and a dusty black coat and trousers, bounded into the room. "Well, I'm off. Just wanted to say you can trust my discretion; doctors are used to keeping their lips clamped."

Miles exchanged a glance with his mother. "Why?" he asked. "What's wrong with her?"

Leaning very closely, he hissed, "Nothing that seven more months won't cure!" When he received only a blank look in response, he added, "She's with child, milord. But she won't be the first in that situation, a single girl like her. Such a shame, though."

As he bustled off, Miles felt his mother's horrified eyes on him. "Well, it's not *mine!*" he declared.

"I knew that," she said, her voice betraying relief.

He gave her a prolonged look. "I think we'd better go upstairs and question our guests, whoever they are."

"No need for that," said the woman they had known as Mrs. Highton as she rounded the stairs and entered the parlor. "I'll explain about what the physician just told you. My daughter's sleeping now, and I don't want to disturb her."

"Your daughter," Miles said, scorn heavy in his voice. Why didn't this woman look more ashamed? "You'll be interested to know I've just received a letter that says *Mrs. Highton's* daughter is in a convent."

"Oh." She smiled weakly. "That would be my other daughter."

Miles's gaze grew more chilly. "Your *other* daughter."

"Please let me explain." She sat and motioned for the others to do the same. "When my husband made his agreement with Lord Beaumont, he did so because of concern for our daughter, Desiree. Very early in her life, she decided she wanted to become a nun. Mr. Highton couldn't accept this. She was his only child, and he wanted the line to continue."

She might as well be speaking a foreign language, Miles thought. He understood nothing and believed less.

"I should tell you that my other daughter, Carissa, the one who is sleeping upstairs, is the child of my first marriage," she said. "My first husband died in a shipwreck. Let me assure you that Carissa is married to a fine young man who has allowed her to participate in my plan at great sacrifice to himself."

Miles stood impatiently. "Your plan . . . that would be the one where Carissa impersonates Desiree, am I following you?"

"Why, yes. Do understand that I was going to

tell you everything before we left; well, I would have had to, wouldn't I?" She laughed lightly, lost in her own world, while the viscount and his mother exchanged frowns. "But now this unexpected blessing has happened—you don't know how long Carissa and James have wanted a baby; oh, she is far older than she looks, by the way; that's why we knew she could pass for Desiree's age even though she's nearing five-and-twenty; she took after her father in her youthful looks, not I, unfortunately!—I'm sorry, I'm rambling because I'm so very excited about becoming a grandmother!"

"Mrs. Highton." *If Mrs. Highton is your name,* Miles added silently, although her expression was so sincere he found himself believing her despite all the subterfuge. "May I ask *why* Carissa has been pretending to be Desiree?"

Her hands fluttered to her cheeks. "Oh. Of course you'd want to know that. Ha! I am become a rattle-top, but just wait, Elise, until it happens to—well. The reason we came was to find out what kind of person you are, Lord Beaumont. I fear my second husband was a very tyrannical man. He didn't care about Desiree's feelings, but I do. I thought if Carissa and I visited and discovered what you were truly like, we would spare Desiree unpleasantness if you weren't suitable. But I'm happy to say you've exceeded our expectations! Now when Carissa and I go to the convent, we'll paint a lovely picture of your life here and perhaps Desiree will change her mind and not take her vows."

Miles shook his head as if to clear it. "Mrs. Highton. Why did Carissa not visit as herself? Surely you and she could form an opinion just as easily through honesty."

"But it was important to know how you'd treat *Desiree*, the woman to whom you were betrothed," she explained as if speaking to a child. "By pretending to be Desiree, Carissa was able to spend much more time with you than she could have as a future sister-in-law. We wanted to know what you were like over time, you see; that's the only way you can truly understand someone. Had you been violent or a gambler and knew we were coming to make a judgment, you might have been able to hide that behavior from us, whereas if you were secure in the match, you'd be more likely to behave normally."

She pulled at her collar nervously. "And there was one other thing. Desiree's Catholicism. As you are Anglican, we feared that might cause a conflict before you had a chance to become fond of one another."

"And what if I'd lost my heart to Carissa? What then?"

Mrs. Highton laughed. "My Carissa is much too wise for that. She knows how to keep a man at a distance; any attractive woman does. But had she detected anything too warm in your regard, she would have spoken."

Miles folded his arms, thinking that Roslyn in her glory could never devise such a wild scheme. "You've gone to a great deal of trouble for nothing. I'm very much in love with someone else. I can't marry your daughter—*either* of them." Hearing his mother gasp, he turned. "I'm sorry, Mother. I'd rather lose an arm or leg than the estate, but I can't live without Roslyn."

"Oh, Miles," she said, tears welling. "Oh, my dear."

At that moment Mrs. Highton stood, looking very grave, one hand resting near her throat. "Then that is the sign Desiree was seeking. When I told her what Carissa and I planned, she argued against it. Finally she said, "Very well, Mother, do as you wish. God will show you what He wants for me.' " She swallowed. "And I suppose He has."

Miles stared into her eyes for a long interval and knew she spoke the truth. "You have only to tell us when we should leave," he said, the words scraping his throat raw.

"Lord Beaumont, Desiree will be making a vow of poverty when she becomes a nun. She's already disclaimed interest in your estate, and I have no need of it. Far be it from me to interfere in the destiny of others anymore, although it was my husband's greatest wish to manipulate everyone even from the grave. Marry your Roslyn and give Elise many grandchildren to love. Live your lives in the home of your ancestors, and live them well."

Drawing in a breath, Miles swept her hands to his lips. He embraced his mother as she broke into happy tears, then, unable to bear another second of delay, ran through the hall and to the stables, where he fumbled the saddle onto Damon's back and rode like a fury. As he neared the road dividing Oakwood from Misthaven, he saw Roslyn jump the hedge on Northwind. Returning her horse to his stable.

No. Returning *home*.

He urged Damon faster. Roslyn caught sight of him, saw him wave, saw his exuberance, and her face dissolved into hope. She leaned forward, racing toward him. The distance between them narrowed. He called her name and laughed as he rode forward to claim her, his love, his future.

His life.

BOOK YOUR PLACE ON OUR WEBSITE AND MAKE THE READING CONNECTION!

We've created a customized website just for our very special readers, where you can get the inside scoop on everything that's going on with Zebra, Pinnacle and Kensington books.

When you come online, you'll have the exciting opportunity to:

- View covers of upcoming books
- Read sample chapters
- Learn about our future publishing schedule (listed by publication month *and author*)
- Find out when your favorite authors will be visiting a city near you
- Search for and order backlist books from our online catalog
- Check out author bios and background information
- Send e-mail to your favorite authors
- Meet the Kensington staff online
- Join us in weekly chats with authors, readers and other guests
- Get writing guidelines
- AND MUCH MORE!

**Visit our website at
http://www.zebrabooks.com**

More Zebra Regency Romances

Put a Little Romance in Your Life With
Fern Michaels